JOURNEY INTO DARKNESS

a story in four parts

part 1

On the Eve of Conflict

part 2

Up From Corinth

part 3

Across the Valley to Darkness

part 4

Toward the End of the Search

TOWARD THE END OF THE SEARCH

the conclusion of the story

BOOK 4 OF **JOURNEY INTO DARKNESS**

written by

J. Arthur Moore

Author's Note:

Journey Into Darkness was begun some years ago. It is finally being written at the request of Charley French, one of several campers who heard the story while on camping trips with the author. Learning the original story had not been worked on for some time, he offered to represent the main character if the author would continue to work on the story. So for him and others who have enjoyed the telling of *Journey Into Darkness* this book is written.

Another camper, Michael Flanagan, suggested the format of the story. On behalf of the many young readers who do not like thick books, he felt several smaller books would be more appropriate. Therefore the story of *Journey Into Darkness* is told in a series of four books.

All photography is by the author. Duane Kinkade is represented by Charlie French; Johnny Applebee is represented by David Rowland; Jonah Christopher is represented by Christopher Oswald; and Jaimie Fowler is represented by Devon Christman. All youngsters, except Devon are participants in camping programs directed by the author. [note: Richie was not available at the time, so 25 years later, his daughter, Devon, represents Jamie.]

This is a work of historic fiction. An intricate blend of fact and fiction, the thread of experience of the fictitious boy soldier runs through the fabric of a very real war and its historic violence exactly as it happened.

This book was printed in the United States of America.

Rev. date: 04/08/2013

To order additional copies of this book, contact:
Xlibris Corporation
1-888-795-4274
www.Xlibris.com
Orders@Xlibris.com
133372

Dedication

Toward the End of the Search is dedicated in His love to Charley French, David Rowland, Christopher Oswald, and Devon Christman, each of whom has helped by becoming forever a part of the story through the photographic material, and to all who have enjoyed its telling and shared in the adventure of its creation.

Duane Kinkade

Johnny Applebee

Jonah Christopher

Jamie Fowler

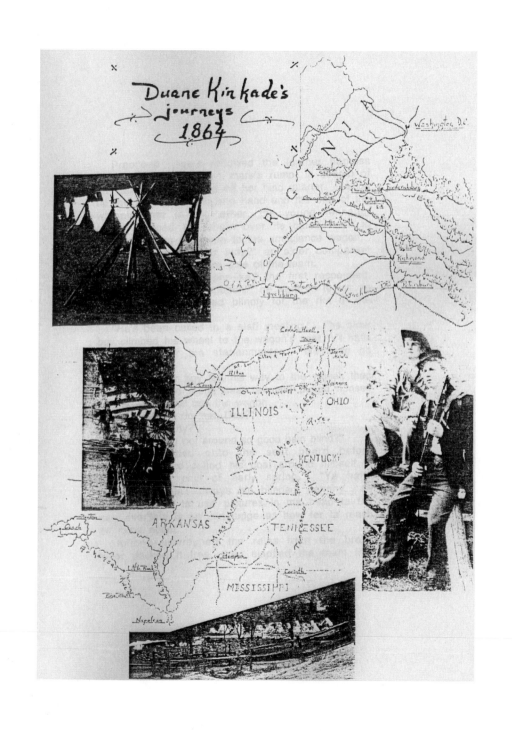

Practiced fingers followed the leather harness strap across the brown mare's rump, in search of the trace chain hanging off her hind quarter. Taking up the chain link with one hand and the end of the whipple tree in the other, the young teenager quickly looped the chain over its catch hook to finish attaching the mare to the ambulance wagon.

"You done on your side?" an older companion asked from the opposite side of the team.

"She's hitched proper-like," the first responded. "Where's Captain Marshalton?" he went on to ask as he turned and reached blindly for the rim of the front wheel.

"He's been called to a staff meeting." The older boy climbed his wheel to the wagon's seat. "I have the papers for the stationmaster. We're to go without him."

The younger boy felt his way to the wheel, then reached for the metal seat rail and pulled himself up the wheel and into the wagon.

"How do you do that, Dee?"

"What, Johnny?"

"How do you get around so good bein blind?"

Duane settled onto the seat board before responding, and pulled his coat around himself to ward off the chill of early spring. "Ya hafta rememb'r, I ain't always bin blinded, Johnny. I's learnin maself ta use pictures in ma head ta the way ever'thin is an' kin judge as how fer ta reach an' move about."

Johnny unwrapped the reins from the brake lever, kicked it free, then slapped the team into motion. Trace chains jingled as the whippletrees swung taut and the team pulled the vehicle into motion.

Both boys were dressed in worn blue uniforms of the II Corps of the Federal Army of the Potomac. They had been in winter camp around Brandy Station, north of the Rapidan River in northern Virginia, since the two armies had ceased hostilities in early December 1863. The elements of General Lee's Army of Northern Virginia were scattered for miles throughout the country to the south of the river. The Union Army's camps covered nearly ten square miles in the general vicinity of the Brandy Station stop of the Orange and Alexandria Railroad, which served as the army's supply center and shipping link from Washington.

In the months since Gettysburg, Duane had passed his thirteenth birthday, been reunited with his friends, Johnny Applebee and Daniel Marshalton, and journeyed with them to join the 20th Indiana before the closing activity of General Meade's move against Lee's army at the end of November. The last three and a half months had been spent in the extremities of boredom of winter camp. For some, the encampment had been a time for festivity, balls, horse races, and whatever competitions or methods of gambling the imagination could devise. For most it had been exceedingly boring, broken only by the routine of drill.

During the months of winter, many enlistments ran out and newly drafted companies arrived. The ranks of new arrivals were swelled with a number of professional bounty jumpers who filled in for draftees for a price, then disappeared during their first picket duty to find another who would pay. Thus, several Fridays saw hangings or firing squads as deserters were caught and executed to discourage others from trying to leave.

In mid-March, General Ulysses S. Grant was put in charge of all the Union armies and came from the west to be near General Meade and the activity of his army. Just Wednesday of this week nearly ended, General Meade had reorganized the Army of the Potomac into three corps of which the 20th Indiana was part of the Third Division of the II Corps. General Hancock, who had been seriously wounded at Gettysburg, had just returned to duty and was given charge over the corps.

It was a raw final Friday in March of 1864 as the ambulance wagon made its way north through the Federal encampment toward the expansive stacks of supplies along the sidings at Brandy Station. Duane's brown eyes saw nothing, but his ears bore witness to the activity about the moving wagon. Johnny chattered away sharing a running account of all he saw. Three years Duane's senior, Johnny had continued to serve as a medical aid and was now actively assisting Captain Marshalton in routine sick call duties. Duane had pushed himself to learn everything he could to assist as inconspicuously as possible. Blind soldiers were unheard of and there were many who frowned on Duane's presence. More than once, a court decree naming the captain as his legal guardian was all that kept the boy in the army.

"I smells horses an hears 'em too," the blind youth observed. "Could be thet cava'ry camp agin?"

"Sure is," his friend confirmed. "They've made wooden floors on top the mud for their horses to keep their hoofs dry. The troopers are standing about with nothing better to do than stare at us going by."

Duane turned his face toward the smell and feel of the camp, smiled, and waved. Some waved back.

"You did it again," Johnny stated. "It sure keeps them guessing."

"Sher does," Duane smiled to himself as he faced ahead once more.

The wagon continued its journey through the vast sea of camps. Thousands of tents and log cabins were laid out in streets, rows, or neat clusters. There were quartermaster camps with rows of wagons for ferrying men and supplies from place to place. There were wagon parks where wagons waited by the hundreds for the spring campaign. Everywhere there were wooden walkways to help the men keep out of the mud as they traveled afoot about the camps. In various parts of the encampment, craftsmen plied their trade. Carpenters were building pontoon boats for the army engineers to use in bridging the rivers for the spring advance. Wheelwrights, carpenters, and harness makers were busy building or repairing wagons in their field shops about the camps while blacksmiths and farriers worked from mobile forges and wagon-based shops.

Nearly an hour had passed before the boys approached the cluster of buildings that was Brandy Station. The air hummed with activity as work crews unloaded rows of box cars lining the sidings, to stack and arrange crates and barrels for distribution to the quartermaster camps of the various army corps. Another train, newly arrived, stood on the main track while its crew prepared to switch the loaded cars for empties from one of the side tracks.

Johnny guided the wagon to the station office before halting it and setting the brakes. "Wait here," he instructed his friend as he took his paperwork and climbed down the side.

Waiting on the wagon seat, Duane listened carefully to the surrounding noises to develop a sense of activity and to orient himself to the setting. The shout of orders, the grating of crates on wagon beds, the jingle of chain and harness from impatient horses, the rumble of steam from the locomotive—all filled the air with the discordant sound of purposeful activity. Alert ears picked up a quiet sound of furtive feet and hands sliding along the wagon's side boards.

"What is it ya be wantin?" the boy asked, turning to face the invisible stranger.

There was a moment of silence. The approaching colonel paused.

"Say yer piece," the boy stated calmly.

"Well I'll be damned," a tenor voice responded. "You are blind."

"What if I is?"

"You ain't fit to wear that uniform. Simple as that. This army doesn't allow for blind soldiers." The voice was frank. There was no tone of hostility or threat, just a plainly spoken stating of fact.

"I'm called Dee," the boy introduced. "How might I call you?" He offered his hand where it should be right by the sound of the voice.

The man took the offered hand. "I am Colonel Russell of General Haye's staff. I see by the clover on your cap that you're also with the II Corps."

"Yes, Sir. I'm assigned to Captain Marshalton, assistant surgeon for the 20th Indiana." The boy's voice was firm as he controlled the pain of fear that was growing within.

"Your courtesy is noted, Corporal. But you have no business in the army and I shall personally see to it that you are sent home. Good day, Corporal."

"Yes sir, Colonel."

The man went on his way and was soon lost in the activity around the station. Johnny returned from within the station and climbed back up to the wagon seat.

"What's wrong, Dee?" he asked, taking up the reins and releasing the brake. "You look like you've seen a ghost."

The wagon began to move as the youth guided the team to the left.

"There was a Colonel Russell from General Haye's staff as said he was gonna git me sent home cause a my bein blind and not fit ta be in the army."

"He can't do that!" Johnny exclaimed.

"I do hope ya's right," Duane said.

"There are others who've tried before. None of them got their way."

"Guess yer right."

The two rode quietly as Johnny drove the team to a designated area stacked with incoming medical supplies. All about were the voices and clatter of intense activity as dozens of wagons came and went with their assigned movement of materials.

"There goes the U.S. Mail," Johnny observed as the square-looking, canvas-covered rig rattled past, drawn by a team of dappled greys.

"Thet's gotta be the most movin wagon in the camp," Duane added.

"Here we are," Johnny changed the subject. "Let's get loaded and out of here."

The older youth handed the papers to a supply agent as the man turned from a customer just finished, then climbed down to start loading. Duane climbed around the seat into the wagon bed where he rolled and tied the canvass side and carefully positioned himself to stack the load. He'd done this before and had become very proficient at the task. Johnny simply identified each item as he lifted it to the side boards and Duane knew how to grab it and place it in the wagon. The loading began.

"Bandages."

The crate hit the board edge and the boy lifted it in, sliding it against the far side.

"Bandages."

Again the crate was placed.

"Morphine."

The case was loaded.

After a half hour of working throughout the yard's various stacks of materials, the job was completed and the wagon cover lowered into place. Duane hopped down from the tail-gate, felt his way around the vehicle, then climbed back up to his seat. Johnny made a final check to be sure the wagon was secure, then he, too, climbed back up to the seat. Taking up the reins for the last time, he released the brake and turned the team south for the trip back to camp.

*   *   *

A fire crackled in the rough stone and log fireplace with its barrel chimney on the outside. The end of the wall tent had been set snugly against the fireplace construction like many others along the company streets of the regiment's camps. This section of the camp housed hospital personnel, bandsmen, and teamsters. Nearby was Colonel Taylor's headquarters. The colonel commanded the 20th Indiana. Captain Marshalton was next door. Once again, Duane and Johnny shared quarters with the medical supplies. They also had a makeshift table and pair of chairs which had been fashioned from empty crates during the first month of winter camp.

Duane sat on his cot, slowly sewing a separated seam in a shirt. Johnny perched on a chair near the fire reading a medical book he had borrowed from the captain.

"How am I doin?" the younger boy asked, holding his work for his friend to see.

Johnny laid his book aside and went to inspect the job. After careful study, he replied, "Won't be quite so drafty, but sure is awful looking. There's still a piece to go."

"Jest so's it's bein done," Duane said. "Don't 'spect I'll be too good fer a long time, yet."

Johnny returned to his reading, but sat instead and stared at his friend. Finally he raised a question that had bothered him a long time.

"Dee, remember us passing the corps' mail wagon?"

"Yea."

"How come you've never written your pa a letter?"

The needle paused mid-stitch as the question caught the boy by surprise. He thought to find the answer.

"I reckon it neve' come ta mind ta try," he finally replied. "Ain't neve' writ ta no one regular-like b'fer. They's no relations ta home an I neve' figger'd fer mail goin ta the enemy." He thought a minute. "Ya really think a letter could go ta the enemy side?"

"Why not? There's lots of Union men with family in the South."

"Would ya put ma words ta paper fer me, Johnny?"

"Sure thing. Let me find a pencil and sheet of paper."

Laying his sewing aside, Duane hugged his legs and rested his chin on his knees. The warmth of the flames flickered on his face. Rummaging through a box of requisition paperwork, Johnny found a pencil and a sheet of blank paper. Resting it on his book, he announced he was ready.

"Dear Pa," Duane began. "I hope this letter gits ta ya so's ya knows as I is alive. I ain't thought ta write b'fer 'cause it neve' come ta mind it'd eve' find ya. If this here letter does git ta ya, I's in Virginia with . . ."

"Not so fast," Johnny interrupted. "I ain't the army's fastest writer."

Together the two continued to establish Duane's location and to explain how he had gotten there. The writing was finished and addressed to Captain Andrew Kinkade in the 13th Arkansas with the Confederate Army in Tennessee.

"We'll put it in tomorrow's mail and see what happens," Johnny stated.

"I cain't wait!" Duane exclaimed. "How long ya think it'll take ta git there?"

"Don't really know. Maybe a couple of weeks."

Johnny stuck the letter in the cover of the book and let it protrude so he wouldn't loose it.

Outside, footsteps approached the tent. The door flap was pushed aside as the captain entered.

"Evenin, Boys," he greeted.

"Evenin, Dan," they chorused.

The man approached the fire and settled on a chair.

"Eny news from yer meetin?" Duane inquired.

Warming his hands in the heat of the flames, the man answered, "General Grant's still in Washington, but due to arrive here tomorrow. I figure it won't be too long before the spring campaign begins. The officers have been told to send their families home tomorrow."

"That would sure seem to mean we're to move before long," Johnny agreed. "Any more from that Colonel Russell?"

"Not yet," Dan replied. "Nevertheless, Dee must continue to do all he can to be as useful as possible so no one can complain that he's a liability to the army."

"We wrote a letter ta my pa," Duane beamed.

"Good idea, Dee. I wonder why we never thought of it before?" the captain stated.

"Jest ain't give it no thought," Duane answered. "But how will it git ta the other side in this war?"

"It should go, shouldn't it?" Johnny added.

"I'll tell you what might help," Dan offered. "I have to see the chaplain for some testaments that's been asked for. I'll give him your letter and he can send it throught the churches."

"Thanks, Dan," Duane said.

"Here's the letter." Johnny pulled the folded paper from the book on the table and handed it to the captain.

"By the way," the man added as he stood to go. "Your little sutler friend, Jonah, was around selling some maple sugar fresh from Pennsylvania. I bought you a bar so you could sweeten your salt pork. Said he'd be by again to see if you had any odd jobs for hire."

"Eny idea when he'll be back?" Johnny asked.

"Reckon to see him near sun-up tomorrow." The captain crossed to the door flap. "Keep warm."

"Yes, Sir," the boys chorused.

As the door flap fell shut behind Captain Marshalton, the mellow tone of a bugle cut the night air with **TATTOO**. It was immediately picked up and joined by regimental buglers throughout the camp, as they signaled it was time to settle in for the night.

Duane concentrated on finishing his sewing while Johnny opened the book to complete the page he had started.

After fifteen minutes, the older youth closed the book and laid it quietly on the table, then turned to watch his friend. Duane was carefully examining his work with finger and thumb tips, running gently along the stitching to see that it was closed. Satisfied the job was done, he patiently guided the needle point under the last stitch to tie off the thread.

"Does it look ta be done?" Duane held the work up to be examined.

"It'll do," Johnny answered. "Time to turn in."

The shirt was laid across a barrel end at the head of the cot. Both kicked their shoes under their beds and stripped to their johns. As Duane climbed in, Johnny blew out the lamp before he, too, climbed under his blankets. After some squirming, both settled into comfortable positions.

"What's yer thinkin fer tamorra'?" Duane asked.

"If Jonah shows up," Johnny suggested, "we could use him for you to practice some nursing chores like bandaging, giving water, and writing information. You got to be real good to help at the field hospital. We can also practice folding blankets and cots, and packing things for the wagon."

"Sounds ta be a real dull day." Duane shifted onto his side.

"You know what Captain Marshalton says."

"Yeh, gotta prove maself ta be a' use."

The two lay quietly for a moment. Outside, the night was momentarily filled with the soft strands of **TAPS** as the last call echoed through the countryside.

"Night, Dee."

"Night, Johnny."

Hot coals crackled in the fireplace. Quiet settled over the encampment. As the two teenagers drifted off to sleep, so too did the nearby quarter of a million souls of the opposing armies, scattered across the landscape.

* * *

"You sure you know what you're doin?" ten-year-old Jonah asked. He lay on Johnny's cot, partially wrapped in white bandaging with loose ends hanging in every direction.

"Guess it ain't too good," Duane stated. Frustration edged his voice as he knelt by the cot with an end of rolled fabric in one hand, trying to feel for its position with the other.

"I suppose a wounded soldier wounldn't be too happy. He might even get worried," Johnny observed. "But you've gotta admit, it should give his companions a good laugh."

"Yer sher?"

"Definitely!" Jonah snickered.

Suddenly, the three burst into hilarious laughter. Duane placed the rest of the bandage in Jonah's hand and sat back on his heels, laughing quietly to himself and shaking his head in wonder that he should try such impossible things.

"I think we need to get out of camp for a while," the eldest suggested. "It's too nice outside to stay cooped up in here. Besides, with officers packing out their families today, there's little around here that needs doing."

"Ya think Sergeant Baker will let us take two horses?" Duane asked.

"Sure. Let's go." Johnny stepped to the bed to help Jonah free himself of the wrappings.

Duane felt his way back to his bed, then rummaged for his coat and hat. Freed of fabric wrappings, Jonah sat up and reached for his coat while Johnny banked the fire.

It was mid-morning as the three boys left the tent, gathered Jonah's horse, then wandered over to the open stabling area for the division's supply train livestock.

Jonah Christopher came from Pennsylvania. His father was a sutler who had come into the Federal camps in January. He was assigned to a Pennsylvania regiment where he built a cabin roofed with canvass and went into business selling soldiers and officers anything from tobacco, candy, and canned goods to stationery, some clothing, and cards. Officers could buy whiskey. Some of the enlisted would con it on occasion by impersonating an officer. But prices were twice what they should be and Mr. Christopher quickly became as disliked as most of his lot.

The boy wanted to be a soldier. He was afraid the war would pass before he got his chance to fight. Of slight build, he looked lost in the oversized Union coat and forage cap he wore. One day in late January, the captain and his boys had stopped at the Christopher store to purchase some candy. The boys met at the counter and took to each other at once. Since then, Jonah had frequently ridden the three miles to the camp of the 20th Indiana to visit, and the two teenagers have enjoyed his presence and his constant chatter of news from about the camps.

As the trio approached the open stables, they knew they were near from the sound of a hundred thousand flies buzzing about a mountain range of manure. The smell was awful, perfumed slightly by the mountains of hay and bags of feed. The sergeant allowed them two horses which they saddled quickly for a fast departure from the odoriferous valley.

"Where to?" Duane asked.

"How about southeast to the river and spy on the Rebs!" Jonah suggested enthusiastically.

"Southeast it is," Johnny stated.

As usual, Johnny looped a long lead line from the bridle of Duane's horse over the horn of his saddle. One thing the loss of sight affected unexpectedly was the ability to ride. Unable to see what lay ahead, Duane could no longer anticipate the horse's moves. Still, he could sit his saddle well and Johnny saw to it that there were no surprises.

The three riders struck off toward the course of the Rapidan River near the Germanna Ford to the southeast.

They rode through acres of tent cities and log communities spread over rolling hills and open fields. Stands of oak and cedar were scattered about the landscape as were acres of stumps where trees had been felled to provide for structures, walkways, and roads.

Along the way the riders observed some regiments at morning drill and paused to watch. Stopping near a Rhode Island company, the trio was distracted by a raucous cheering. Turning toward the camp, they saw a large number of men gathered in a cluster. On closer investigation, Jonah pointed out a crated cock bird and they figured there were more in the center of the crowd. Dismounting, the three moved close to the edge of the crowd to watch the excitement. Duane used a thin cane when walking to help "see" where he was going. When riding, it hung from the saddle horn on its own leather loop.

The boys stayed on for a half hour to watch the cock fights and the betting, and to cheer for their favorite bird. When their interest faded, they mounted and continued on their way.

The ride was leisurely, allowing for frequent stops to rest the horses or their riders. The sun was high toward noon as the trio crossed the open ground approaching the river.

Duane reined his mount to a stop and the others did likewise. "Tell me as it looks," he requested.

"There's what's left of a broken-up barn just ahead," Jonah described. "There's a house about a half mile to our left."

"Looks like a broken bridge of sorts off right," Johnny added. "The countryside's pretty open and rolls down to the river's edge."

"Anyone hungry?" Jonah asked. "I packed us some candy."

"Dismount!" Johnny mocked. "There's a fence rail here to tie your horse on, Dee."

As the three settled on the grassy roadside, Jonah handed each a small bag of hard candy. Duane selected a piece, smelled it, and placed it in his mouth. Stuffing the bag in a pocket, he lay back with his hands under his head to rest and to roll the candy about with his tongue as he sucked on its sweetness. His companions did the same.

A distant sound caught the thirteen-year-old's attention. "I hear som'thin ta the rive'," he whispered.

The others looked hard to see what might be there.

"I can't see no one," Johnny whispered from where he stood by the fence, shading his eyes with his hand as he scanned the country along the river bank.

"What's that?" Jonah pointed toward the embankment near the bridge structure.

The oldest youth studied the spot indicated before he replied. "Looks like a patrol on picket duty settling to make a fire."

Duane sat up, rattling his candy into his cheek before he spoke. "Which army?"

"Yanks," Johnny replied.

For a quiet moment the two studied the distant activity. Suddenly a voice called from across the river.

"Hallo the Yank Patrol!"

"It's Reb cavalry," Johnny discerned.

"Hallo yourself," a Federal soldier replied.

The boys listened to the distant exchange.

"We got tobacco! Ya all got some coffee to spare?" the cavalryman inquired.

"Pound for pound," the reply was called.

"Mind if I cross over?"

"Come on along. Save me from gettin wet."

As the boys watched, a grey-clad rider forded the river with his sack of tobacco to meet with the blue-clad infantrymen and work out a trade. A few minutes later, they exchanged goods and the rider rode back across the river. Once safe on the opposite bank, the soldiers from both units waved farewell and the cavalry patrol rode off.

"Did I tell you about the company I heard of on picket duty in a old cabin?" Jonah asked as he watched the riders depart.

"Don't remember as you did," Johnny replied as he turned his attention to his candy and settled on the ground with his back against a fence post.

"There was this company on picket duty that stayed in an empty cabin each day outside their lines and returned to their camp each night." The youngster sat down on the grass to explore his candy selection while he shared his story. "One morning as they arrived at the cabin, they saw it was taken by Reb cavalry and was about to have a shootout when someone had a idea. The Rebs used the place at night and the Yanks at day. So they figured each could go on havin his turn and agreed to leave a warm fire goin for each other."

"Sher is a heap better 'n shootin each other," Duane observed. "Thet would be sech a waste as no one would git no good of it."

"You two want to go on down to the river?" Johnny asked.

"Don't reckon as it'd be too good a idea," Duane thought. "Could be they'd fret we might a seen 'em tradin an wanta be sher as we couldn't say nothin."

"Yea," Jonah agreed. "And me and my pa ain't exactly popular with a lot of fellers."

"Think they'll see us?" Duane asked.

"We're pretty easy for them to see," Johnny stated. "But they're probably too busy fixing something to eat." He rose to his feet. "Just the same, it wouldn't be a bad idea to head back. I'd hate to have to leave in a hurry."

Jonah selected a candy and popped it in his mouth, then stood and stuffed his bag into his coat pocket. Johnny guided Duane to his horse. They all mounted, then turned away from the river to start back toward camp.

*   *   *

March drifted into April. Pay day passed and with it came new stock at the many sutler tents. Jonah was kept busy by his father and had not been around in recent days. With the onset of the new month came an increase in drilling and the realization it wouldn't be long before the neighboring armies would march against each other.

The Federal soldiers were well rested and well supplied. Sickness had taken its toll. Even so, the troops were ready, though some were still determined to cut and run.

Duane and Johnny stood shoulder to shoulder in company formation along with musicians, teamsters, and others from the surgeon's staff. The regiment was gathered along with everyone else of Major-General Birney's Third Division. Before the troops, some fifty yards distant, stood Jason Trible and Thomas Kirkland. The two men, in their late twenties, had taken money to fill in for draftees, then had run out while on their first guard duty assignment. Behind each man lay his coffin beside an open grave.

In front stood a company of riflemen and their captain. The regimental chaplain was addressing Trible and Kirkland.

"What's happenin now, Johnny?" Duane whispered.

"Their chaplain's talking to them," came the soft reply.

"Cain't hear nothin."

"Me neither."

The two stood fidgeting uneasily along with the other thousands in the division. "I hate this. It's such a waste," Johnny stated.

There was the clatter of rifles coming off the ground at the command of "Make ready!"

"Take aim!" Hammers clicked back and fingers rested on triggers.

"Fire!" Two dozen rifles clattered in volley, spitting fire and a rolling billow of smoke.

The air reverberated with gunfire, then was caught up in a collective breath of surprise.

"Damn!" one of the bandsmen exclaimed softly.

"What?" Duane wondered.

"They only shot one of them!" Johnny explained. "The other's just standing there."

"Reload!" the captain ordered.

Again the commands were given. Again the volley was fired. Again the man remained standing, after staggering back from a bullet in his arm.

"Run, damn you!" another intoned quietly.

"Why ain't he runnin?" the boy asked. "Ya think they'd shoot him in the back?"

"I don't know, Dee," the bandsman replied, glancing at the boy.

Again the company fired. This time the man fell dead.

"Oh, God," Johnny whispered. "That other fellow ain't dead neither. He's getting up."

"And the one they just shot's still movin," another observed.

"Ain't it been enough?" Duane asked. "Why ain't they callin it even an quit this. It's jest a plain murderin waste."

"The captain's taking his pistol and going to finish them off," Johnny whispered.

There was a very distinct click as the revolver misfired. The man was shaking terribly as the two condemned men twisted about on the ground in agony. Again the captain fired and the gun roared as the shot slammed through the man's chest and blew him dead against the ground. The other awaited his fate in agonizing distress. Once more the revolver spoke. But the shot was not fatal. Finally, the officer put the barrel to the condemned man's head and fired.

The final gunshot echoed and reechoed about the landscape and within the minds of the witnessing division, numbed by the horror they had just watched. It was one thing to shoot the enemy in battle or to die an agonizing death from the wounds of battle or from disease. But this! These were two of their own.

The burial detail placed the bodies in their boxes and lowered them into the ground. The dirt was shoveled in and the graves closed over. Nothing was placed to mark the graves. Deserters were not permitted grave markers. Jason Trible and Thomas Kirkland were gone forever, except in the minds of those who witnessed their passing. There they would be remembered until each soldier's dying day.

Following the execution, the regiments returned to their drill fields to practice the rest of the morning. The bandsmen gathered for a practice of their own. Duane, Johnny, and other non-combatants gathered to watch and listen.

Hours slipped by.

During the afternoon Joshua Bacton, a nineteen-year-old drummer from upstate New York, continued in another teaching session with Duane and Johnny.

"Here's a cadence we used in our community band back home." He played a catchy rhythm, part on the drum head and part on the wooden rim. "Now you try it, Dee."

Duane had his old drum strapped on. It had been repaired with new skin heads and replacements of damaged rope and leather tabs. He caught the cadence to perfection and didn't miss a beat.

"How's thet fer doin as yer done."

"You're real good. You've a great ear for music. Maybe you can play with us sometime when we do a sit-down for the regiment." Joshua's interest in music was far greater than any political interest in the war. He didn't believe in the fighting, but was willing to help musically and when his turn came in the litter brigade to bring the wounded in to the hospitals.

"Johnny," he turned to the older teen, "do you think you're ready to try a drum roll?"

"Show me how," the youth requested.

Duane slipped his drum from his shoulder and passed it to his friend, adjusting the strap for greater length.

"Hold your sticks like this," Joshua instructed.

Duane took his friend's hands and worked the fingers into the correct position.

"Now watch what I do and count each tap."

It was awkward. Yet he managed a fair copy of the tappings.

Captain Marshalton approached the trio. The war had aged him. He looked like a man in his forties. His dark hair had grown down over his collar and was ragged at the edges. The man paused to watch the lesson before interrupting with his own concerns.

"Not bad, Johnny," Captain Marshalton complimented. "But I'd rather you take up the harmonica. This army does not need another drummer boy."

"No need for worry, Dan. I've seen enough damage to keep from volunteering," the boy assured. Jamming the sticks into his belt, he found a barrel for a seat to await the captain's news.

The other two paused and turned their attention to the doctor.

"What's everyone looking at me for?" Dan asked.

"Jest waitin ta hears what fer ya come by," Duane answered.

"It's not good news, I'm afraid." The man propped his foot on a box and leaned on his knee. "Remember that colonel you ran into last week, Dee?"

"Sher, Colonel Russell of General Hayes' staff."

"Well, he's taken his objection to General Hayes who has come to General Ward. The general wants to see you, now." There was concern in the voice as the captain stood to depart.

"Will ya be with me, Sir?" Duane stood.

"I will, Dee. I have the court papers. Let's go."

"I'll put the drum back," Johnny stated. "Good luck with the general."

"Thanks, Johnny." Duane reached for his guide stick which lay on the ground at his side, then stood to go.

Turning to the captain from the last sound of his voice, he approached to where he felt the man's presence at his left elbow.

"See you boys later," Marshalton stated.

Duane placed his hand on the man's wrist and the two departed for the brigadier-general's headquarters.

*   *   *

Brigadier-General John H. H. Ward was seated in a camp rocker at a table under the canvass canopy which projected from the front of his wall tent. Long hair curtained the perimeter of a balding head, ending with a slight curl just above his collar. A walrus mustache added to the dark gaze and a full face to give an authoritatively stern appearance. He was a large man and amply filled his chair. With his concentration focused on a game of chess with his staff secretary, the general was unaware of the approaching youth and surgeon.

Some who were watching the game looked up. The captain and the blind corporal paused respectfully to wait and be recognized. Some with the general exchanged whispered remarks. Thus aware of some new presence, the general glanced up to see the cause of the whisperings.

"One moment, Captain," he acknowledged, then returned to his game.

The moment stretched into fifteen minutes. The game progressed slowly.

"Won't you be seated," a staff officer offered pointing to an empty chair and a stump.

"Thank you, Lieutenant," Marshalton replied. To Duane he whispered, "We're going oblique right. Chair is left of stump. The lieutenant is close to the right."

The boy used his stick to check the way for objects and kept a sense of closeness to the captain at his left. The two proceeded slowly, Duane reaching out cautiously with his sense of feel for any awareness of air pressure change in his distance from the captain and approaching figures. The general glanced up from his game to observe as the boy paused near the lieutenant.

"I ask yer pardon, Lieutenant, but I ain't wantin ta step on yer shoes 'r knock inta ya."

The man stepped aside. The boy and the doctor continued to their seats. Duane searched out the stump with his stick. When his toes found it, he checked its surface with his hand, then turned and settled on it.

"You do very well, Corporal," the general spoke.

Duane jumped to his feet.

"Relax," General Ward stated. "You may be seated."

Duane lowered himself cautiously. Captain Marshalton settled in the chair.

Leaning back in his rocker, the general opened the conversation. "Corporal Duane Kinkade, is that correct?"

"Yes, Sir."

"Tell me, Corporal, how does a blind boy get into this army?"

"I weren't blind, Sir. I've bin in this war since Shiloh an did good service the whole time since, 'cept when I bin laid up some from sickness 'r woundin." He sat straight on the stump, resting his walking stick across his lap.

"How did you lose your sight, then?" General Ward rested his hands on the arms of his chair.

"I was in the fightin at Gettysburg when a powder charge blew up in ma face. It were a long while fer I was healed up ta travelin. Now as I's fit agin, I kin do a bunch a thin's ta he'p out fer the doctorin."

"Why don't you go home, Corporal? There's many a lad stuck a toe out to a cannon shot and lost his foot just so he could go home. Why are you still here?"

There was a moment of quiet as Duane tried to seek the answer to the question from within himself.

"I's scairt," he whispered. "There ain't none a ma family left an I know's how it is here. I ain't knowin what I'd find at home an' I'm plumb fine as I is."

"Where is your family?"

"Ma was kilt by raiders an Pa went ta fight in the war. I left ta find him an ain't yet."

General Ward leaned forward in his chair, resting his elbows on his knees. "Haven't you written him."

"At first, Sir, but the letter neve' got ta him."

The general stood and paced to the side to stare out over the camp. He turned, with hands clasped behind his back, and faced the captain. "Captain Marshalton."

"Yes, General."

"Why is this boy with you?"

"He's my legal ward until we find his father."

"What steps are being taken toward that end?"

"He has written to his father through our chaplain who has routed the letter through the church in hopes of getting directly to his father's unit."

"Why should that be necessary? Just send the letter through the regular mail."

"The boy's father is in General Bragg's army, Sir."

There was a moment of stunned silence. "But that's the Confederate Army, Captain," the general finally stated, leaning his hands on his table near the chess board.

"Yes, General," Marshalton confirmed. "Corporal Kinkade is from Arkansas."

There was an exchange of shocked stares from the officers who had been listening to the conversation.

"What in God's sake is a Rebel cripple doing in my brigade!" the general exploded.

"With all due respect, General Ward, he has proven himself on the battlefield and off in bravery and in trust."

"In whose army, Captain!" The general had risen to his full stature and moved to the front of the table facing Duane with his hands placed authoritatively on his hips.

"General Sheridan's command, Sir," Duane stood. "General Ward, Sir, I ain't wantin ta cause ya no kind a embarrassment an' I ain't wantin fer yer staff here ta be upset none. I ain't in this war ta kill Yanks 'r Rebs, either one. I only want ta find my pa. I done my part he'pin those as was wounded an' I done a share in the killin—both Yank 'n Reb alike. I do feel a heap prideful fer the fi'st an' damnation fer the killin. But I ain't wantin ta let no one put me und'r if'n I kin he'p it. Fer this present, I only want ta do what I kin ta he'p the captain till he kin see me ta findin my pa."

The statement was firmly made without the rise of emotion or anger. The general stood a moment, then glanced around at his officers to study briefly the reactions on their faces. It ran from strong disapproval to respectful acceptance.

"You may be seated, Corporal," the general stated as he stood a moment longer to study the sightless youth.

Duane resumed his seat on the stump as the general dropped his hands to his side and wandered back to his chair. Standing behind it, he rested his hands on its back.

"Captain Marshalton."

"Yes, General."

"Does General Sheridan know this boy?"

"Since he rode with Sheridan after Shiloh."

There was a restlessness among the staff officers who had been listening throughout the discussion. Some shifted to a more comfortable stance or found a place to sit or lean.

"In light of all that's been learned, and I know there's much more should I ask for detailed accounting, I will allow things to remain at their current status while I review this with my staff. I'll be in touch early next week." The general remained behind his chair as he waited for the two visitors to stand and depart.

Rising from his chair, Captain Marshalton tapped Duane's elbow to signal it was time to go. Then he spoke once more to General Ward. "Would it be appropriate, General, to inquire of General Sheridan in pursuit of a letter of recognition or support on behalf of the corporal?"

"You have my permission, Captain. Such a letter would make my decision much simpler," the general responded. "Good day to you, Captain Marshalton and to you, Corporal Kinkade."

"Good day, General," each returned.

The two departed as General Ward rounded his chair to resume his seat and continue his game. The boy took the doctor's arm and they moved quickly to disappear from the curious stares of the staff officers as they lost themselves in the commotion and movement of the surrounding camps.

Back at regimental camp, Duane returned to his friends and their practicing while Dan retired to his quarters to write a letter to General Sheridan.

*　　*　　*

As the days slipped by and a new week reached its midpoint, Jonah returned. Duane lounged sleepily in a canvass camp chair while Joshua and Johnny lingered in drum lessons on the ground beneath a large oak tree some forty yards distant. An older bandsman, a horn player named Zachary Bennett, had joined them in their musical endeavors.

"Hi," Jonah greeted as he approached the napping boy.

"Hi, yerself," Duane acknowledged quietly, having heard the other's approaching footfalls.

"You heard me comin?" the ten-year-old asked.

"Yeh," was the reply. "Somethin gnawin at ya?" Duane inquired.

"How'd ya know?"

"Yer voice. It sounds as like ya's havin yer troubles."

"You can say as I have." Jonah knelt on the ground beside the chair and took his friend's hand to touch its fingers against a black-and-blue knot on his head.

"What's bin done ta ya?" Duane asked. He ran his fingers lightly across the face in search of other signs of brutality.

"A bunch a soldiers got mad at my pa as the canned meats they'd bought was putrefied. They got themselves all liquored up an' come tore up the business. Pa's broke up bad and the doctor put him to hospital with a cracked head, broken arm, and stove ribs. I fixed up the store best I could and closed it up taday." A tear or worry slipped free. "Dee, what am I gonna do?!"

"I reckon as ya kin stay here tonight an Johnny 'n me'll go back ta he'p ya best we kin. Besides, I ain't so sher as ta what'll come a' me. General Ward's likely ta have me shipped out fer being blind." He put a comforting hand on the younger boy's shoulder. "Could be as you 'n me'll both be cut loose ta fend fer arselfs."

"It ain't right," Jonah stated indignantly. He stood to find a seat for himself and stopped motionless as he saw, in the distance, a rider headed along the tent street in their direction. "There's a general on his horse ridin this way," Jonah whispered.

"I figer'd as he'd send a orderly to the captain with a letter," Duane mused aloud.

"He's not from here," Jonah added. "And I think he's cavalry, cause there's yellow on his uniform."

The boy found a barrel and moved it beside Duane's chair as a seat. The two waited in quiet expectation as the others continued with their music, unaware of the approaching visitor.

The officer rode slowly, glancing about the camp at the soldiers in their routine, obviously in search of someone. Eventually he paused in front of the boys. Sensing the presence and hearing the impatient snort of the horse, Duane stood respectfully. Jonah followed his friend's example.

"You aren't Corporal Kinkade, are you?" the officer asked.

"Yes, Sir, General—Sheridan?" Duane wondered.

"Yes, Corporal," he answered, swinging down from his horse as Jonah stepped forward and took the reins.

"But how . . . ?"

"Captain Marshalton's letter." He removed his gloves and tucked them into his belt. "How are you, soldier?" he offered his hand.

"I'm doin okay, General," Duane offered his hand and met the general's. "Would ya like ta set a spell? Jonah here might have a candy with him as his pa's a sutler."

"I'll accept a piece if you're offering," the man took the chair while Jonah searched his pockets for his bag of hard candies.

Duane held the horse during the candy search. The bag was retrieved from a deep coat pocket and offered to the general who made his selection. Duane then settled on the barrel while Jonah made himself comfortable standing with the horse and stroking his neck.

Returning the bag, General Sheridan explained, "I was in Washington on my way here when the letter reached me. Since I was coming down to meet with General Grant and his cavalry commanders, I decided a stop at your camp would help me respond to the captain's concerns. How did you lose your sight?"

"A powder charge blew on the ground near ma feet," Duane answered briefly.

"I haven't seen you since that day at Stone's River. Have you had any luck in finding your pa?"

"I come close. But bad luck had it I was headin the wrong way and neve' did git ta Bragg's army."

"Could be I don't want to hear the particulars of your travels, but it does surprise me that you haven't found your way back to your own people. I must agree with the concern that you really don't belong here. Blindness is a tremendous disadvantage. I recognize you are a good soldier and have done your duty. Knowing what I do of you and of the army's immediate needs for the coming campaign, and of your relationship with Captain Marshalton, I know you will make a contribution to your regiment. I think as soon as your captain can be spared, he should personally see that you are reunited with your own people and sent home."

There was a moment of silence.

"General Sheridan?"

"What is it, Corporal?"

"I know as how yer right. I 'spect as how it got easier ta stay on with thin's as I knew they was then ta try ta git home not knowin how thet would be. I's scairt a not knowin what may be if 'n I was ta go."

"I understand, Corporal. I will recommend that you stay on until such time as Captain Marshalton can be given leave to personally see to your affairs." The general stood to leave.

"Thank ya, General Sheridan." The boy stood.

"You're a good soldier, Corporal Kinkade. My recommendations are based on my personal knowledge of that fact. I wish you well." He took the reins from Jonah. "Thank you for the candy, Jonah." Mounting gracefully, the general waved. "Take care, both of you. And give my regards to the captain."

The two boys stood as the general turned his horse and rode back the direction he had come. Johnny and the two bandsmen approached as they suddenly realized someone had stopped and was gone again.

"Who was here?" Joshua asked.

"It was General Sheridan!" Jonah exclaimed.

"Seriously, Jonah, you expect me to believe such foolishness?" the youth mocked.

"It were so," Duane confirmed.

"What did he say?" Johnny asked.

"Do you believe this, Johnny?" Joshua persisted.

"It's true. We know the general."

"Let's go see Dan," Duanc answered his friend. "I'll tell ya then."

"What happened to Jonah?" Johnny exclaimed noticing the bruised lump on his head.

"Tell ya 'bout thet, too."

"I have to go now, Joshua," Johnny excused. "I'll talk to you about playing again this evening."

The bandsmen watched as the boys headed off to the captain's tent. Then they, too, went their way to gather with the rest of the company for afternoon drill.

*   *   *

The following day the sutlers were ordered out from all the army's camps. Jonah bade his friends farewell and said he'd find a way to pack his pa's business and have it ready for his pa when he got out of the hospital.

General Ward sent instructions to the effect that Duane would stay until Captain Marshalton could be sent on leave to put the boy's affairs in order. General Sheridan's reaction was evident as much was in accordance with his comments to Duane during the previous day's visit.

Serious preparations were set in motion to get ready for the spring campaign which was expected to finish Lee's army and to bring the war to a close. April passed slowly. Finally in the last week, General Meade was notified to advance. The baggage wagons were loaded as the supply trains prepared to get underway. General Grant had been back and forth to Washington on weekly visits as he coordinated the plans of all the Federal armies. Corps commanders increased drill schedules and set about putting their commands into battle trim. General Sheridan stayed on to assume command of the combined cavalry forces which were to operate as an independent force.

The Army of the Potomac was well supplied by way of the railroad connection to Washington. The men were equipped with everything a soldier could want, were well fed, were in their best health, and were in good spirits.

May had begun before the immense wagon trains were ready to roll. Their six thousand wagons would stretch for sixty miles. The roads would have to be clear and the moving army would have to be able to protect them.

Wednesday, May 4th, was a glorious spring day. Wild flowers danced in all their splendor, caressed by a gentle warm breeze. The last of the camps were packed. The three army corps were gathered in ranks. At five o'clock in the morning, the advance was finally underway.

*   *   *

The fragrance of pine scented the air. The blossoms of dogwood splashed the woodscape with patches of white. The thickets of the wilderness crowded alongside the roadway reaching to snag the thousands who passed in their journey toward Chancellorsville. As the army's corps advanced southward, the II Corps moved further to the east to cross the Rapidan River at Ely's Ford. From there it followed the narrow wilderness road toward Chancellorsville. It was mid day when the divisions of General Hancock's corps began arriving at the crossroads where the charred remains of the Chancellor House stood silent against the blue sky, rising above the cloud of dust kicked up by the gathering army.

Dispersing across the open landscape about the ruined mansion, the corps' divisions set their bivouacs for the day. Johnny and Duane pulled their medical supply wagon into line with the others in the brigade's train. The horses were unhitched to be tethered at the horse lines. There the boys left them to graze on the grass at their feet. Returning to the wagon, each took his gear to join the others of their company to make a bedding area for the night and to share a fire for their dinner. Next they headed toward the edge of the woodlands in search of firewood.

As the two wandered the underbrush that skirted the field, someone shouted, "Hey, look what I found!"

"What is it?" another called.

"A skeleton," the first replied.

Several rushed to examine the find when still another announced, "There's one here, too. No. A couple of them!"

"Johnny, where's the house from where we stand?" Duane asked.

"Off behind us a ways," the youth answered as he added another branch to his friend's load.

"No, what direction?"

Johnny glanced toward the sun then responded, "I guess it's north and east of us. Why?"

"I was here at the fightin last year. I was in these woods when they was burnin an' men was dyin. Yank guns was in these fields. My friend, Tod, was wounded here. It were a true Hell with the shootin 'n screamin 'n fires burnin all 'round 'n smoke burnin yer eyes 'n lungs." Duane stood remembering, his mind wandering the battlefield of another year.

"I guess there's a lot of dead that got left behind," Johnny thought aloud.

His friend didn't hear him. Johnny paused to study the landscape and to visualize what most of the men present had experienced.

"What did ya say, Johnny?" Duane suddenly came back.

"Nothing," the sixteen-year-old replied. "Let's get our firewood and get back."

Reaching into the thicket he grabbed a smooth stick and picked it up.

"Oh, God," he whispered.

"What's frettin ya?"

"It's a bone!"

"Yank 'r Reb?"

"Dee!" He dropped the white remnant, then pushed aside the vegetation to see what remained of the body. "Blue uniform scraps, must have been a Yank. It's charred, too. Musta been burned in the fire."

"Sher hope he was gone fer the fire got ta him."

"Yea," Johnny agreed quietly.

A small group of infantrymen passed the boys in their own search for firewood and paused to look at the remains.

Before moving on, an older sergeant remarked, "That's what we're comin to tomorrow."

No one said any more. Some nodded in agreement, then they continued on.

The boys finished gathering their wood and returned to their fire site. Activity continued throughout the countryside as more of the corps' wagon train continued to arrive and other brigades settled in for the day. Fires were made and the air was scented with their smoke and with the aroma of brewing coffee. Many of the companies broke out their shelter halves and two-man wedge tents soon lined acres of company streets.

As the afternoon wore on, activity quieted. The soldiers settled by their fires to cook dinner from provisions in their haversacks. Following dinner, the men amused themselves with gambling, song, gossip from the latest news, and quiet talk and reflections. Joshua, Zachary, and Thomas Siddle shared the fire with Duane and Johnny. Captain Marshalton also sat a spell. Thomas had a guitar with him and was a very proficient player. Joshua also played a harmonica. The five sang some ballads and love songs and one of which Duane had become very fond—**JUST BEFORE THE BATTLE, MOTHER**.

Just before the battle, Mother
I am thinking most of you,
While upon the field we're watching,
With the enemy in view.
Comrades brave are round me lying,

Filled with thoughts of home and God;
For well they know that on the morrow,
Some will sleep beneath the sod.

Farewell, Mother, you may never
Press me to your heart again;
But O, you'll not forget me, Mother,
If I'm numbered with the slain.

Hark! I hear the bugles sounding,
'Tis the signal for the fight;
Now may God protect us, Mother,
As he ever does the right.
Hear the "Battle Cry of Freedom,"
How it swells upon the air;
Oh, yes, we'll rally round the standard,
Or we'll perish nobly there.

The song brought warm memories of his mother and Duane liked to imagine her standing on the porch back home waving to him as he returned, welcoming him back. But the reflection always ended with the image of her headstone in the churchyard with heaps of wild flowers lying at its base and the boy and his dog sitting by the grave to spend time with her.

As the gathering finished the last chorus, the boy lost his voice to an emotional tightness in his throat and simply mouthed the last words. But this was nothing new to those about the fire and they simply paused a moment in silence while each poured a cup of lukewarm coffee.

"Guess we'll be startin early in the morning," Zachary stated.

"Any idea where to?" Thomas asked.

"Captain says we're headed south through a place called Todd's Tavern and beyond," Johnny offered.

"Do you really think we'll get by Lee's army without a fight?" Thomas wondered.

"He ain't like ta give us no more time 'n we's already had," Duane mused.

"I agree," Joshua put in. "We won't see a quiet sunset tomorrow."

Nothing more was said. As each finished his coffee, he wiped the cup to tie it once more onto his pack.

Twilight faded to night.

"Good night," each said in turn.

The fire had dwindled to quiet coals, winking in the gathering darkness. Tree toads and crickets sang their night songs. A billion bits of light danced in the blackness overhead. A soft hum of ten thousand subdued conversations drifted on the night.

"It's gonna be real bad tamorro'," Duane stated as he lay on his back facing the stars.

Johnny rested his head on an outstretched arm as he lay on his side facing his friend and wondering how he would handle the fighting. What would he be able to do being blind? It was one thing in winter camp. But an army on the move and in combat would be something very different.

"I'm guessing you're right, Dee," the older teen responded. "I think it will be the worst yet."

"Night, Johnny."

"Night, Dee."

The two drifted into a restless sleep.

*   *   *

The new day began early. It was still dark as Duane and Johnny hitched the team to their supply wagon and moved it into the line of march. General Hancock had his corps on the move by the time the first faint glow of dawn began to light the eastern horizon. All around the moving column of infantry, the wilderness rang with the cheerful babble of the sparrows and robins and the raucous cawing of the crows. More than an hour after the sun had risen, about seven o'clock in the morning, Johnny and Duane were rattling along in silence when a distant thundering became audible to the northwest.

"It's begun," Johnny stated.

"I know," Duane agreed.

The column continued its advance another mile and a half before it halted. General Birney's division was first in line, so it wasn't long before Captain Marshalton rode up with information. He paused on Johnny's side of the wagon.

"There's a fight developing to the north," the captain stated. "We're to hold here at Todd's Tavern crossroads until decisions are made. You two okay?"

"What fer am I ta do if we goes in ta the fightin?" Duane asked.

"You stay with me helping the wounded behind the lines," Dan replied. "You know how the field pack is arranged and will stay at my side or Johnny's. Okay?"

"Yes, Sir. I'll do ma best," the youngster replied.

"I'll be nearby," Johnny added. "We'll do all right."

For nearly an hour, the troops waited as the activity to the north intensified. Finally orders were received and the division started north on a narrow dirt lane called Brock Road.

As the lead division advanced, the mass of wagons and artillery and manpower quickly clogged the roadway which was hemmed in on both sides by the jungle-like entanglement of the wilderness landscape. Nearing the intersection of the Orange Plank Road, the crescendo of full battle just ahead brought a sudden urgency for action.

It was nearly two o'clock as the division under General Birney was thrown forward to support another Union division that had been in the fighting for three solid hours and was nearly out of ammunition. As the brigades advanced into the the conflict, their first order was to throw up breastworks of log and earth from which to advance on the enemy. The air rang with the riflery of engaged troops to the front, which ranged along the left of the road running north and south, and the ring of axes and shovels in the immediate vicinity. Amidst this frantic activity, Captain Marshalton took his company of medical and non-combatants to set up a field station behind the second line of earth works near the crossroads. They quickly found themselves overrun with wounded as men from General Getty's division, in combat since the morning, overburdened their own surgeons in search of help. The sounds of battle subsided for a while, replaced by the sounds of intense preparation for a combined assault of several divisions.

In the meantime, Duane found himself with all he could handle trying to do a competent job of assisting the wounded.

"Bandages!" someone called.

Reaching in the pack where bandaging materials had been placed, the boy grabbed a roll of cloth and held it toward the sound of the voice. It was taken from his hand.

"Alum!"

Duane withdrew the stiptic and passed it.

"Bandages!"

"Tourniquet!"

"Bandages!"

The chaotic press for materials drained the supply quickly.

"Empty!" Duane called.

Joshua rushed forward a fresh pack as he moved back and forth with those transferring materials from the medical supply wagons.

Others assigned to the litter brigade rushed wounded from the front who were within reach of friendly lines. A mile behind the lines a clearing was found and a field hospital was set up as a gathering place for those who could be evacuated by ambulance. The captain had set up an operating table with planks straddling wooden horses, just off the side of the roadway near the entangling undergrowth of the woodland.

After two hours of preparation and maneuvering, the attack began. Federal forces advanced through the dense tangle of brambles and vines on either side of the Orange Plank Road. Several pieces of artillery had been placed on the road itself, but they were of little use in the thickets of the Wilderness. After covering about four hundred yards, the Union front was struck furiously by a withering fire from the waiting Rebel lines. Hell exploded with searing fury and the screams of pain, the shriek of the high-pitched Rebel Yell, the clattering and ear-splitting waves of riflery firing in line, the shouts of orders, the beating of drums, the frantic whinny of horses, and finally—the crackle of flames. A thick smoke from gunpowder and the burning woodland began to roll up through the wilderness to burn the eyes, nose, and throat; to seer the lungs.

The fury of the battle spread over a half-mile front, constantly widening as more troops were pushed into the conflict. The field medical operation worked at a feverish pace to keep up with the incoming wounded. Brigade first aid operations were scattered all along the backside of the fighting. But their numbers were insufficient to handle the flood of casualties.

The wounded came on their own if they could walk. Some were assisted by others less seriously hurt. Some were carried in blankets by their comrades or on litters by members of the litter brigade.

Duane held his own at first, working from memory out of the field packs of supplies. Then the pace became frantic and he froze in a panic.

"Dee! What's wrong!" Zachary called, seeing the boy sitting motionless.

"I cain't do it! I ain't no good!" the boy shouted back.

"Here, be useful," the musician responded. "Help me hold a tourniquet on this guy's leg."

Zachary dragged Duane to the side of a wounded soldier, then grabbed the boy's hands and placed one on the bloody remains of a shattered leg and the other on the stick in the bandage.

"Is he dead?" the boy asked.

"No," the horn-player answered. "But he's unconscious. He will be dead if you let go. I'm going to tie down the tourniquet while you keep it in place."

The conversation was shouted over the din of battle and the confusion of activity behind the lines.

The battle wore on into the evening before the action subsided. Throughout the action, the line remained stalled. No ground was gained or lost. The casualties continued to flood the temporary aid stations. The seriously wounded went to the surgeons' tables as fast as possible. Minor injuries received little or no attention due to lack of time. The dying were left to die. If someone had time, they might get some water or a last friendly word. When possible, the chaplain wandered among them and sought to give some solace or to write down their names for later identification.

Lamps were lit as darkness fell, and the aid stations continued their work through the night. The soldiers on the line slept under arms if they could, or sat up, waiting for the new day's fighting. Some crawled through the entangled thickets in search of water only to find themselves in the enemy's lines. Their search for water became a search for safe refuge.

As Duane continued his work, he became acutely aware of his limitations and struggled to adapt to whatever chores he could carry out successfully. But the situation kept demanding the impossible and he was forced to improvise and to stretch the fine tuning of his senses.

"Oh God, help me!" a voice begged.

"How?" the boy asked, crawling on hands and knees in the direction of the voice.

"My leg, it hurts like hell!" the man moaned between clenched teeth.

"I cain't see ta do nothin," Duane stated.

"Damn it, Boy! Get someone who can!"

"Ya kin see, Sir?" He dragged a medical pack around to a convenient location at his side.

"Don't play games, Boy!" The pain-filled voice was tight.

"Jest tell me what yer leg is like 'n I'll do as I kin." The boy's voice was steady and authoritative. To the wounded soldier there was a confidence, comforting enough to let the boy try.

Pushing himself up on his elbows, the man described a shattered knee, laid open to the side. Gingerly feeling his way with gentle fingertips, Duane folded the torn flesh, chips of kneecap bone, and shredded pants leg fabric back across the top of the knee. Then he wrapped it carefully to hold until the surgeon would get to it, and splinted the leg.

"I ain't got nothin much fer the pain but a sip a' brandy," the boy apologized.

"That'll do fine," the man stated. "You're okay, Boy. Thanks." The words came slowly with painful difficulty.

The man took a sip of the brandy. Duane moved on at another's request to help with others of the wounded.

Night wore on past midnight. Though the line of battle was generally quiet, preparations behind the breastworks went on as ammunition wagons were brought up, generals checked their lines, and the wounded were returned to duty or loaded into ambulances to be moved further to the rear. Finally, around two in the morning, Duane and the others found some time to collapse and rest.

Johnny found his friend lying among the wounded.

"You okay?" he asked.

"Yeh. Jest a heap wore out," Duane answered. "Eny news 'bout the fightin?"

Johnny settled on the ground beside his tired friend. "It seems part of Lee's army is in front of us about a mile down the road, and another part is facing V Corps and VI Corps up on another road. This wilderness makes it real hard to get any place. But General Hancock is preparing for a really early start in just a couple hours." He paused to study his friend, covered with dirt and blood from the long day's work. "You sure you're doing okay?" he asked again.

"I do hope so," the boy responded. "I ain't so sher as I's bein a' much use ta no one. 'Tain't much I kin do 'cept as some'ne is doin with me. I gotta make the wounded ta he'p if there ain't no one else 'bout, jest so's I kin git him fixed up fer ta hold him ov'r a spell fer the doc."

"I'll try to work with you for a while, Dee," Johnny offered.

"Sher would be a comfort," Duane accepted.

"Let's get some rest," the older youth suggested.

He stretched out on the ground between his friend and one of the wounded. Both were asleep in an instant.

*   *   *

The time for sleep was short. Predawn glow had just begun to redden the eastern horizon when gunfire erupted to the north west. It was 5 AM as the battle was renewed. Within minutes, a clattering of musketry announced the advance of skirmishers as General Birney's division moved to the offensive. More than 20,000 Federal troops advanced against General Lee as the noise of conflict awoke Duane and Johnny. Suddenly the woods exploded with the roar of violence as the mile-wide wave of battle surged relentlessly forward.

During the next two hours the Federal line continued to push forward. At first, the two youths worked together as the ebb tide of wounded stumbled to the rear in search of help. Along the Brock Road from the north of the aid station, troops and artillery flowed southward into the battle. The immediate crossroads hung thick with the rolling dust of their passage and the noise of the moving masses and their vehicles, spurred on by the shouts and commands of their officers.

Word came that the battle line was nearly a mile to the front of the breastworks.

"Dee," Johnny shouted over the din of activity, "you stay here with Joshua and Micah. I have to go forward with the brigade!"

With that, Johnny was gone. Wagons of ammunition and medical supplies rumbled down the road. Duane heard all this feverish movement of battle and worried in the back of his mind that Johnny would be killed. He was sure something terrible would happen. Nevertheless, he continued to help dispense materials from supply packs and to follow the guidance of the two bandsmen as he assisted them in whatever way they needed.

The roaring tide of battle continued in the distance for most of the morning. For a time, numbers of Confederate wounded and prisoners were brought in as the Union line had collapsed the Rebel line and forced it back upon itself. Then, as the sun neared its high point at noon, there came a distinct crescendo in the fighting. The tide was turning and the Confederates were pushing the Federals hard toward their own breastworks. A great rush of activity spilled from the woods as retreating infantrymen dashed to the rear and a vast horde of wounded was brought in.

Shortly after noon, the retreat was complete as the Federal forces returned to their breastworks and Johnny rejoined his friend. The smell of burnt powder became strong in the air as it blended with the smell of blood. The ground about the aid station was littered with the mix of wounded, both Union and Confederate.

"The surgeons are having a real rough time of it," Johnny observed as he helped Duane distribute stiptics, bandages, and splints. "Just as fast as one poor fellow is cut and moved another is on the table. The blood is so deep, the ground at their feet is a red slime. The bloody pieces of bodies are stacked in piles knee high."

"Damn it ta Hell, Johnny, but this be one time I's glad I cain't see 'n I really ain't needin fer ya ta say as how bad it is. The pain an' screamin 'r bad 'nough. Ma nose an' ma ears is tellin a real heap a horrifyin sufferin. I reckon too, as I hears Reb voices in the wounded likewise."

Hundreds were occupied with the task of treating the wounded. The fighting continued along the first line of breastworks as the brigades of General Birney's division continued to withdraw to the line of defenses. The momentum slowed and the battle line settled in a stalemate just a few hundred yards from the field medical activity. By mid afternoon there was a welcomed lull in the fighting during which General Hancock directed a rearrangement of troops for greater strength and in preparation of a concerted charge to be mounted in the late afternoon.

As fast as they could, the non-combatants at the aid station loaded the wounded who could travel onto ambulances to be transported off to Fredericksburg.

"Hey, Dee," Johnny called. "What was your brigade at Gettysburg?"

"Thirteenth Alabama. Why?" He tied off a bandage knot, then stood to face the voice.

"There's a wounded Reb here from the 13th, a kid named Matthewson."

"Jamie!" Duane shouted. "Is he bad hurt?"

Johnny moved to guide the boy to the lanky youth who lay among the wounded. "Looks bad."

"Dee, is't really thet yer alive?" the faint voice called weakly.

"I is fer sher," he knelt beside the sixteen-year-old. "Ya got back from the fightin thet day?"

"Yeh," pain cut him short.

Duane remained beside his Confederate comrade while Johnny left to continue his work.

The youth went on, "I come to near evenin an saw as they was takin in wounded. I made like I was dead an waited fer night ta git back ta the company. I sher did think as ya'd met yer maker when I last saw ya layin in yer blood." A fit of coughing overcame the wounded youth.

The younger teen sought his friend's face with his fingers and explored gently to see how bad he was hurt.

"Hey," Jamie whispered, "it tickles. What ya doin?"

"I cain't see, Jamie. Lost ma sight thet day when a powder charge blew in ma face." He felt the sweat and dirt of battle and the long curls of dusty hair, but no indication of a wound. Wait. There was a trickle of blood at the corner of his lips. "How bad hurt is ya?"

"There's one as burned ma arm. Another grazed a shoulder. Wu'st one's in ma gut—broke a rib an' got ma innards. Weren't so bad fi'st off. But the Yanks had already gone by an' the only way out an' not bein shot agin, was ta the Yank side. I started ta walk 'n only went a few yards an' had ta crawl. Some with a litter carried me out."

"What's this?" Duane asked, wiping blood from his friend's mouth.

"Banged inta a tree branch durin the fightin. Kinda dumb, I s'pose."

Duane slipped his hand to the bloodied shirt around Jamie's abdomen. Ripping it open, he gently explored the wound, first where the bullet entered; then, by sliding his hand around the older boy's side, the exit hole on his back.

"Oh God! Thet hurts!" Jamie gasped in sudden pain.

"I'm gonna put some bandagin ta hold ya tageth'r, Jamie," Duane explained as he searched his pack for more fabric.

"It ain't wo'th yer tryin, Dee. I know I ain't got much time left. Jest stay with me an' talk some." The wounded youth fought hard to control his voice and to keep the pain from taking over.

"Sher, Jamie," Duane agreed as he gently withdrew his hand from the pooling blood beneath his friend and laid the front of the shirt back across the broken body. "But I ain't wantin fer ya ta die." His voice cracked.

"I ain't a'fear'd none, Dee. I ain't wantin it neith'r, but I knows it's a certain." His voice quivered and a tear slipped free to course its way through the powder which blackened his face. "Jest stay with me a piece."

As the two continued to talk and Duane learned the fate of some he'd known, the hour slipped away. Suddenly, at four o'clock, the air was rent with gunfire as a fierce Rebel charge burst toward the first line of breastworks. The Union line exploded in destructive volleys of riflery and thunderclaps of artillery fire.

The two teenagers shook at the sudden explosion of activity. They were quickly enveloped in the smoke of battle as a breeze blew the sulphurous cloud in their direction.

"Kin ya see how fer the fightin is?" Duane asked.

"'Bout two hundred yards," Jamie answered.

As the battle erupted all along the Brock Road defenses, the woodland once more burst into flames. The wind blew them toward the Union defenses and soon Jamie reported to Duane that the Federal breastworks had caught fire.

"The Yanks is fallin back an' ar people 'r comin through the fire ta the wall!" Jamie described while the bullets whined overhead. "The two armies ain't twelve paces apart shootin each other through the flames," he continued.

Shouts of orders, the roar of cannons, the rattle of frantic wheels, the whinny of horses, the raking volleys of musket fire, screams of pain and panic, rose to a numbing intensity.

"Get down!" Johnny shouted as he rushed to Duane's position. "We're holding them!"

The leading edge of attacking Confederates mounted the breastworks, but the fighters were cut down as fast as they came. Finally, the men of General Birney's division were rapidly reinforced as new troops were brought into the conflict. The line held. Frantic activity behind the line kept everyone busy who was able to help as the new flood of casualties fell in the immediate front. Eventually, the fighting subsided as the sun sank low in the west and twilight dimmed the woodlands. A crackling red glow moved eerily through the wilderness. As the fighting ceased and the moans of the wounded rose on the air, fires raced about the underbrush. Moans turned to screams. Scattered gunfire popped about the wilderness as pockets in the clothes on the dead and wounded, filled with rifle cartridges, ignited, and the charges exploded.

The troops settled warily as the wagons raced about to re-supply ammunition and caissons were brought in with fresh munitions chests for the artillery. The work among the wounded was constant. Hundreds had gathered and lay about the area waiting to be attended. Once more, the nurses and non-combatants worked into the night.

Duane took a break around midnight and asked Joshua to guide him back to where Jamie lay.

"Sorry I bin so busy, Jamie," he spoke as he knelt. "Want some water?"

There was no response.

Duane reached out to be sure his friend was there. His hand touched a shoulder. But it was hard as rock. His fingers searched for the face.

"This ain't the right one, Joshua," Duane stated, as he felt the cold hard flesh and the soft curls of hair. "Damn this war!" he exclaimed quietly to himself. "Damn it all ta Hell!"

*   *   *

The fighting in the Wilderness had ended. The following day, Saturday, saw only sporadic activity. A fog hung over the battlefield, mixed with smoke and the stench of burned and decaying bodies. The dead were buried. Ambulance trains clogged the roads to Fredericksburg.

Joshua helped Duane to find a quiet glade alongside the Orange Plank Road where the fighting hadn't cut down the trees or burned the landscape, where a small brook bubbled along, where wild flowers danced in the spring breeze to splash the green grass with their color. There the two dug a clean three-foot-deep grave in the soft soil, taking care to save the sod from its top. Jamie's body, carefully folded in a blanket and wrapped in a tent half, was lovingly placed in the ground. The dirt was laid back in and the sod neatly placed on the top.

"Could ya make a small map ta tell where he lays, Joshua?" Duane asked, after the work was completed.

"Sure, Dee. You hold the shovels for me."

Joshua took a piece of paper and a pencil from his pocket and made a quick sketch of the glade. He paced the grave's location from the edge of the road and from a cluster of dogwood saplings. The measures were marked on the sketch and the date was added, May 7, 1864. He gave the paper to Duane who carefully folded it and slipped it into his pocket. He would put it with the one possession of Jamie's which he had kept, his cap pouch.

The two took their tools and returned to the crossroads.

That night, the army completed preparations and began to move southeast toward Spotsylvania Court House.

*　　*　　*

Guiding his work with his left hand, Duane carefully dusted the sergeant's bleeding scalp with alum. It would help the blood to clot and allow the man to be sent on in an ambulance before further treatment was administered. All about the smoldering line, the troops had settled to sleep by the road. The day had been spent gathering the wounded and burying the dead. Blue or grey, it made no difference. All were equal in their need for attention. At one point in the smoking embers of the wilderness, five hundred from a single charge were buried in line where they had fallen. Yet, as night fell, hundreds of wounded remained in the field.

The boy finished administering to the sergeant as he wrapped a temporary bandage around the bloodied head. Others were at hand to direct the wounded man to a waiting ambulance.

"It's time to pack up," Johnny stated as he joined his companion.

"Ya got ar gear?" Duane asked.

"It's in a supply wagon with Dan's gear."

It was nearly 8:30. The last light of day was fading to night. As the two moved toward the wagon, others were clearing the area of all remaining wounded.

"Give way to the right," a voice called on the road.

Advancing from the north was a large column of troops, headed south on the Brock Road. A small group of men was passing to the front along the right side.

"It's General Grant," Johnny stated. "We're moving towards Richmond. He's not going to retreat." There was surprise in the youth's voice.

A great burst of cheering filled the air as the general was recognized and the soldiers along the line realized these past days of fighting had not been in vain. The army would not retreat.

Grant was obviously not pleased at the noise as he spurred his horse, Cincinnati, and rode swiftly by in stony silence.

"What corps is this?" someone asked.

"General Warren's V Corps," came the reply.

Orders were passed for General Hancock to hold his position until the rest of the army had passed behind his lines, then prepare to follow the march southward. The two boys leaned against the side of their wagon to watch and listen while the corps marched past. It was hours before the road was clear and II Corps was to form up and move out.

"Make ready," Johnny instructed.

The two climbed to the wagon seat and prepared to move with their brigade.

As the corps moved south toward Todd's Tavern, the distant night echoed with three high-pitched yells from ten thousand throats. Lee's army was also on the move.

*   *   *

Thick dust and slow-moving troops delayed the movement south. Periodically, the wagon would be forced to halt. Nearing Todd's Tavern, the entire column was stopped by two divisions of Union cavalry, asleep in the road. As Duane and Johnny sat waiting on the wagon's seat, they were overcome by sheer exhaustion and fell asleep where they sat. It was six in the morning before the leading corps was able to resume the march. Distant gunfire, barely audible on the morning air, signaled the beginning of new fighting.

It was nearly 9 AM when Hancock's corps managed to arrive at Todd's Tavern, having been the last to leave its line of defense in the Wilderness and the last in the line of march on the Brock Road. There, most of the corps waited while the distant conflict unfolded and some divisions were sent on separate missions. Birney's division finally moved early on the following morning when General Hancock sent it and two others to cross the Po River to the south and attack the flank of the Confederate left. At 6 AM three pontoon bridges over fifty feet long each were set in the water. The troops and artillery crossed over. It was evening before the division was in position to attack, and it was too late. Recalled during the night, the division withdrew the following day. On the way back, it was attacked by a division of the Confederate Army. The Confederates were repulsed with the Union suffering heavy casualties and the loss of one field piece which became jammed between two trees. Once more the woodland burst into flame and many of the wounded perished in fires. Duane remembered their screams, the smell of smoke, the crackle of the fire, the currents of hot air, the stench of burning flesh, as they rode the wagon in retreat.

The II Corps was returned to position on the Union right by late afternoon. At seven in the evening, General Birney's division was sent with part of the V Corps to attack the Confederate defenses. The attack faltered.

Three days had passed since the night march south along the Brock Road. The heat had been oppressive. The division had been continuously on the move. The medical resources had been strained to their limits as more than twenty thousand soldiers had been killed or wounded in the six days of fighting since crossing the Rapidan River at Ely's Ford the previous week.

*   *   *

Heavy rain mixed with hail pelted the boys about the head and shoulders as they worked to hitch the horses to the wagon. Protected by rubber ponchos and cap covers, the two finished hooking the harness chains. Movement was hampered by the darkness of night and the severity of the weather. The night was raw as the temperatures took a sudden drop during the evening hours.

The storm had come up during the afternoon of a relatively calm day. After the heavy fighting of the previous day, most of Wednesday had been spent planning and moving. Once again it was time to move as General Hancock prepared to take advantage of the stormy weather to move his corps around to the center of the Federal line in preparation for an assault on a salient of the Confederate center.

"You would think these generals had learned their lesson by now," Johnny muttered as he settled on the seat and unwrapped the reins from the brake lever.

"How da ya mean?" Duane asked, grabbing the seat while the wagon rattled into motion to join the others in line.

"They keep giving Lee time to set his line and Lee keeps doing just that—building defensive works and trenches. They're lined up right with artillery put right and our generals keep sending charges against them only to get everyone blown to Hell!" Johnny's voice bore a strain of emotional frustration and anger.

It was 10 PM as the corps moved around the back of the Union line. Johnny guided the wagon into its position of march and the rest became routine. The rain and hail poured down on the moving troops as others in place along the way huddled by drowning fires with rubber ponchos or gum blankets draped across their shoulders. Some wore their tent halves as capes. Others tried to pitch their tents and crawl under the folds of canvass which served only to puddle the run-off in the mud where their occupants sat. It was a pitiful sight as the tens of thousands endured the wretched weather.

"Sher do hope this storm ends come mornin," Duane wished.

"I don't think it will," his friend returned. "The air's turned downright cold and raw and it seems like it means to stay that way."

"I 'spose thet means tamorra's work'll be put off?" The rain rolled off the rubber folds across the boy's shoes and into puddles in the wagon bed.

"No chance," Johnny stated. "This General Grant means to fight no matter."

The two rode on in silence as the rainfall continued in torrents and the raw cold crept through their clothing. With the movement of troops and vehicles, the road turned to a thick mud and sucked at feet and wagon wheels. Progress was increasingly more miserable. Finally, in the early hours of Thursday morning, the corps was in position and all was in readiness.

General Hancock established his headquarters in a convenient farmhouse. The troops were placed in line of battle in the woods opposite a creek which ran in front of the house. The Rebel defenses lay less than a half mile to the front. As the rain continued to fall and a thick ground fog gathered, Captain Marshalton and his company prepared to set up field medical facilities as close to the front as they would be able to get. A full field hospital was already in operation a little over a mile west at the Alsop barn and house on the Brock Road.

Now there was the waiting. No one slept. Nerves were on edge. The work about to begin was expected to be very heavy. Dan had agreed with the boys. This practice of assaulting entrenched enemy positions was predestined to fail in the end leaving only the high cost in human lives.

The rain continued to fall. The fog and mist thickened so that it was impossible to see one's own feet. The appointed hour came and went as the thousands waited in massive formation, fifty ranks deep. The general determined that visibility was too limited. From where he sat on his horse, he could not see the bottom half of the men around him. All was lost in the swirling mists.

Duane and Johnny watched the silent mass, perched quietly on their wagon seat. Captain Marshalton waited on foot, standing beside the wagon with the non-combatants gathered in ranks nearby or on other wagons and ambulances. The divisions were poised—bayonets fixed, no caps on their rifles—waiting the signal to advance. Finally, at 4:30 AM, the brigades moved forward.

The enemy fortifications which lay ahead began with an abatis made up of limbs and branches woven into one another along a line of pointed pine and pin-oak pikes, in front of which was a ditch. Behind this line were the trenches, banked in front with earth over a wall of fence rails and logs creating a height of about four feet on the back side. Along the top was placed a head log, one that was raised above the rest just high enough to allow a musket to be inserted in the space between it and the rest of the wall.

General Birney's division advanced along with General Barlow's. The men moved swiftly and quietly. They emerged from the woods, crossed a stretch of open ground, and swarmed into the enemy works. Using their rifles as clubs, and fighting with pistols, swords, and bayonets, the Federal troops battled fiercely and were soon in possession of the trenches. Caught by surprise, the Confederates retreated or surrendered. Three thousand were taken prisoner.

"Damn that was fast," Johnny commented from a vantage point near the edge of the trees, as the enemy prisoners were passing to the rear.

"Ain't a whole lot a shootin," Duane observed as he stood beside the older youth with a supply pack in hand.

The captain approached—a ghostly apparition in the misty torrents. "Were we wrong," he asked, "when we concluded this was a lost cause?"

"I figure they'll get us back," Zachary suggested standing with his arms around a folded litter.

The distant conflict was little more than far-off shooting and indistinct shadows in a swirling fog cut by the slanted torrents of rain. It was soon lost as the attacking troops continued to advance beyond the first earthworks to the inner line of defense. Suddenly an intense thunder of riflery exploded on the air. It spread and grew louder. Word came back that a Rebel countercharge was driving the two divisions back to the outer trenches. The divisions of the VI Corps which were waiting in reserve were ordered forward.

The action was an hour old as the walking wounded began swarming to the rear. Duane went to work at the captain's side as he passed the materials for the surgeon to do his work. The table had been prepared under a canvass canopy and was quickly occupied by a large corporal in his thirties who had taken a bullet in the face. It had shattered his jaw and passed through his shoulder. Marshalton began his task to salvage what he could while Duane passed materials as requested.

"I need a sewing needle and thread." The man spoke loudly to be heard above the pounding rain bouncing on the canvass overhead.

Duane fished them out of the surgical case.

"I have 'em," he announced.

Within minutes the sergeant was gone and a young lieutenant was in his place. The man was pale from loss of blood, and shaking with fear. His left arm had been shattered by a mini-ball and the splintered bone protruded just above his wrist.

"Amputation," Dan announced as he directed the litter bearers to stand by.

Duane ran his fingers along the edge of the table of implements until he found the familiar shapes of the amputation knife and saw and a tourniquet. Another put a cloth over the wounded man's mouth and nose and soaked it with chloroform. Captain Marshalton took the tourniquet which the boy held up and quickly tied it above the wound to cut off all bleeding. Next he took the knife, slipped it through the flesh and against the bone beneath the muscle tissue. With a flick of the wrist he deftly cut through from the bone outward, laying the open tissue clear of the bone. Trading tools, he applied the saw and, in a few quick strokes, completed the separation. The artery was tied shut by knotting a string around it and the tissue of the stump was pulled over with needle and thread. All was finished in less than three minutes and the patient was returned to the litter bearers.

While work progressed at the table, the wounded lined the area. The advancing VI Corps had to push its way around the returning tide to clear the wooded area and move toward the front. It was nearing 6 AM as the second assault made its way forward to a marsh of long grasses where the men fell to the ground to await further orders. After being swept by a murderous enemy fire, they rose up with a loud cheering and moved on.

The noise of the conflict swept across the stormy terrain and hung in the ears of those at the aid stations. Chaos reigned as the wounded returned, reinforcements went forward, and artillery and ammunition advanced to support the attack.

Tens of thousands of Confederate and Union troops fought over an area the front of which would hold a single brigade. As the mass of troops fired volley after volley into one another, the men in the fronts fell by the score. The combatants fought in ankle-deep mud, their faces layered and crusted with powder from biting open the paper charges to load their guns. Barrels became so hot that ram rods were fired as powder ignited spontaneously. The bodies fell so thick in the trenches that the dead and wounded had to be pulled out to make way for the fight to continue. The bottoms of the trenches ran red with blood. The mud on the slopes shed sheets of red water. The intensity of the gunfire shredded the head logs as a partial battery of artillery was brought up by the Union attackers. Double loads of cannister mowed down the front of the Rebel line and tore through the oak trees behind them. The cannons continued their work until every horse was slaughtered and every artilleryman cut down.

Throughout the day, the battle roared and the slaughter continued. Ammunition cases were carried forward by pack mule where they were dropped along the line. The company officers broke them open and distributed the rounds to their men. Those who survived to carry the fight fired over four hundred rounds apiece. So intense was the shower of lead that the carcasses of the dead animals and the bodies of dead soldiers were stripped of their flesh and their bones were shattered by the fury. Sometime during the middle of the afternoon, the oak trees fell with a thunderous crash, cut down by the torrent of gunfire.

As evening approached, more troops from II Corps moved up to relieve those who had been fighting throughout the day, allowing them time to reorganize and to take time to eat something. Darkness came; the storm and the fighting wore on. Captain Marshalton was exhausted and bloodied from hours of surgery. Stripped to the waste, he had had time only between patients to wipe his implements on his apron, then begin again. Duane had stayed at his side and survived the ordeal only with the assistance of Johnny and others who had kept the supplies coming and had stepped in when blindness interfered. The ground was covered with bits and pieces of amputated body parts. At times it had been necessary to shovel them aside to make room to continue working. The air stank of blood and gore. It stank of burnt powder and vomit and death. The moans and screams of the wounded rose on the torrents of rain and the constant thunder of the battle just ahead. An eerie glow lit the landscape from the lanterns hung about the surgical areas and from the flashes of gunfire, like lightning on the horizon. A constant motion ebbed about the landscape as wounded came in, relieved troops returned, supplies went forward, and ambulances were loaded and sent off into the night.

Finally, near midnight, General Lee began to pull his troops back to a newly built line of defense. A quiet began to settle. Still, one segment of the line remained in conflict for another two hours. Then it, too, ceased. The dominating sound of uniform constancy was the rain. It continued to slash through the trees and drench the mass of humanity. The work of the surgeons slowed. Men could take so much horror before they became numbed and eventually collapsed from the strain. Some stopped to rest while others tried to continue the work.

A new sound wore on the night. Somewhere in the Confederate line, a band played **THE DEAD MARCH**.

"Come on!" Zachary called. "Our band is forming up."

As the strains of the march faded into the rainfall, the immediate air reverberated with **NEARER MY GOD TO THEE**. The two bands continued to alternate with **THE BONNIE BLUE FLAG** followed by **THE STAR-SPANGLED BANNER** followed by **DIXIELAND**. Finally, the Federal band closed with **HOME SWEET HOME**.

Duane lost track of his work as the music played on his mind. He hadn't cried in months other than to mourn Jamie's death, his emotions somewhat numbed by the carnage. But as he listened and remembered people of long ago, a tear slipped free and tracked through the dirt on his face.

The last strains of music faded into the constant splash of the rainfall.

Duane staggered from the surgeon's table as he was relieved, in search of a place to drop.

"Come with me," someone offered.

The boy took a friendly hand which led him to a nearby wagon.

"Thank ya," Duane said as his guide disappeared.

Running his hands down the rim of a wheel for reference, the boy eased himself to the ground. He tripped over the edge of his poncho as he walked on it with his knees, crawling beneath the wagon bed, then collapsed in the sheltered mud. Struggling for a moment to find a comfortable position in which his rain gear didn't pull at him, Duane eased himself across the rubber garment, then lay his head on his arm to slip into the peace of sleep.

A quiet settled across the countryside. Fields and woodlands were lit by dim circles of light which glowed softly in the continuing rainfall. There, the medical teams worked their miracles or lost their individual struggles to the ravages of warfare. The moans of the wounded were drowned by the constant rush of rain. An occasional scream of pain pierced the night as a surgeon's patient cried out. The exhausted soldiers slept where their work for the day had ended. All around lay the dead, their grotesque forms frozen by death's stiffness. Along the line of battle, their hands had been cupped by the living to form a holder for cartridges in death. In the trenches they lay in heaps, as many as eight or ten in a pile. In the sleep of death or exhaustion, the human forms which carpeted the battlefield were bathed by the constant rain as they rested peacefully in the quiet of the night.

*   *   *

Four more days passed before the rain ended. Except for General Birney's division, much of the time was spent in move and countermove as troops and equipment trudged through knee-deep mud. For the time, however, there was no major engagement. The mud and weather made it impossible.

Monday afternoon saw sunny weather and rapid drying of mud and rain puddles. General Birney's brigade had remained out of action since the assault on the Bloody Angle of Thursday last. The troops had set a temporary camp and generally found time to rest. Duane sat by his fire, carefully feeding the fuel by sensing the fire's position from the sound of its crackling flames and the feel of its heat. Twenty-five-year-old Corporal Siddle was breaking up firewood at his side. Johnny and others were out collecting more. Light footsteps approached.

"Hi, Dee," the young voice greeted. "Can I cook supper on your fire?"

"Jonah!" Duane exclaimed. "How is it yer here?" He lost track of the fire. "Ouch!" The youth quickly drew back his hand and dropped the stick of wood.

"I'll get it," Thomas volunteered.

"Thank ya," Duane acknowledged. He stood and addressed the sutler's boy. "Ya was sent out two weeks back. Why fer ya here now?"

The boy stood awkwardly, a guilt-ridden half smile tugging at his mouth. "You see," he began, "I started to leave when some officer came by and thought I was lost from the II Corps because my cap has a II Corps clover pin on it, and he asked if I was lost and I said yes, and he showed me where to go, and I ended up in the army's supply train. Some one complained I was too young, but they kept me on anyway." The youngster shifted his stance nervously. "Can I sit with you?"

"Sher," Duane stated. "But I ain't got no extra rations."

"I got food. See?" He dug into the pockets of the coat he wore and brought out candy and canned meats. "I'll even trade you some."

"I ain't got but biscuits and salt bacon, and some coffee beans ta brew."

"Okay." Jonah approached his friend and reached out for a hand. "Here." He pressed a tin of meat into the ash-dusted palm.

"Thanks," Duane took the offering. "Walk me ta ma tent ta git ma thin's. Johnny an' the others'll be back in a few minutes."

"Don't get lost," Thomas called as the two went off to get Duane's haversack.

All about the field and wooded area, the company camps of the division were active with preparations for supper. Coffee beans were being ground between rifle butt and rock, firewood was being gathered, salt bacon was being sliced, and fires were being fed. Johnny, Joshua, and Zachary returned with their arms full of firewood.

Dumping his load on the ground, Zachary stated, "That should hold us through breakfast."

"How will it do for an extra plate to cook?" Thomas asked, a mischievous smile pulling the corners of his mouth. "You won't believe who showed up."

"Hi!" Jonah greeted, returning from the tent with Duane at his elbow.

"What in Sam Hill are you doing here!" Joshua exclaimed.

"You'd been sent out," Johnny added.

"What about your pa?" Zachary asked.

"An officer made a mistake an he he'ped 'im," Duane answered. "See thet clover pin on his hat?" The others acknowledged. "Some'n come ta figger Jonah fer a wagon'r a' the II Corps 'n he went 'long with it."

"But what about your pa?" Johnny asked once more.

The blind boy paused when a whiff of smoke blew into his face and he suddenly remembered the fire. His young friend guided him to a place to sit, and the two settled beside the fire.

A sadness crept into Jonah's eyes as he sat and stared through the flames. "When I went to see him at the hospital, he didn't know me. The doctor said he was hit on the head and it addled his brains. I ain't got a pa no more."

The other four joined them as Jonah swung his haversack into his lap to draw out his eating utensils.

The youngster proceeded to tell his story while the mess group started on the food. Joshua ground the coffee and set the prepared pot on the coals to brew. Johnny sliced the slab of bacon and passed the pieces to Zachary and Thomas to start cooking on their plates. Duane opened the cracker box and started to pass out the biscuits. Jonah shared a bag of hard candies while he told of weeks with the supply train, the days it took to catch up with the army, and his search for the 20th Indiana.

As the food cooked and the meal was consumed, the boys told each other of the events they'd experienced in the campaign so far. After all had eaten and the utensils had been cleaned and returned to their haversacks, Captain Marshalton brought his camp chair and joined the gathering at the fire.

"There better be a good explanation, Jonah," the surgeon admonished when he saw the boy with the group.

"There is," Johnny stated as he went on to explain briefly.

"I'm gonna be a drummer boy," Jonah announced enthusiastically, when Johnny had finished.

"I'll teach you," Joshua volunteered. "But only if you stay with the band. I'll not see you going off to get killed."

"I won't get hurt," the boy said in all confidence.

"You're both missing the point, here," Dan intervened. "Jonah already has his job. He's a teamster for the supply train and has a wagon and team to care for. There won't be any heroics."

"This ain't no game," Duane added. "Men really do die out there on the battlefield. Boys die, too."

"Then why were you able to be a drummer boy when you weren't much older than me!" Jonah cried.

For a moment no one spoke. Duane fumbled for a stick of wood and cautiously added it to the fire. Johnny took a moment to inspect his haversack. The captain poured a cup of coffee. Joshua lay back in the grass to await Duane's response. Thomas and Zachary joined the captain in another cup of coffee. Finally Duane tucked his knees under his chin with his arms wrapped around his ankles, and sat remembering the events of two years back.

"Jonah," he began, "I ain't come inta this war fer ta be killin no one. It weren't even real ta me. I jest knew as it was where my pa was 'n if I could be drummer fer a company, I could git ta the war an' find him. I ain't so sher as eny a' us really knew nothin real 'bout war 'til we was in battle at Shiloh. I remembe' the fi'st time I walked in ta thet Union camp an' the docs was cuttin an' the dead was layin in the sun. I was real sick inside an' the captain said as I weren't allowed ta feel bad as I had a job ta do. My beatin a' the drum was real important ta if the men would live. Then we was in the real battle fer the fi'st time. It were a sight ta shake ya good inside, but ya git so worked up an' busy in all thet's doin thet ya stop thinkin.

"I saw a lot a men hurt 'n dyin. But it didn't really git ta me 'til I saw General Johnston git kilt. 'Til he was hit, it weren't real. Next day I was wounded pretty hard an' finally Johnny an' Dan here found me an' got me fixed up good."

The boy paused as his mind raced through the years. "I saw my ma kilt by raiders an' was nigh ta kilt maself, but it didn't seem the same then. I knows better now." Again his mind wandered. "I r'member the fi'st time I shot another soldier, an' he were a Reb. I ain't even thought a'fer it. I jest did it cause he were gonna shoot me."

The small group around the fire watched the youth in wrapped attention as he searched his soul and tried to impress on Jonah the reality of war. Duane released his grip to fold his feet Indian-fashion and to rest his hands in his lap.

"War does thin's ta ya." He faced the direction where he sensed the boy to be seated. "Ya ain't yer real self. It makes ya kill when ya really ain't wantin naturely ta do it. It's a horror ya cain't b'lieve really happens. When we fought at Stone River in the winter an the dead was all 'round in piles, froze in ther own blood 'n gore, my innards up an' I was sick all ov'r the place. This here fightin a' last week was so fierce as men was shootin each other with pistols stuck up so as ta touch each other, an the shootin tore the flesh from the dead an' cut down trees.

"Jonah, war is a 'xcuse fer people ta stop feelin an go fer glory by killin other people. An ya know what they does when they're kilt? They sends messages ta tell ther family as they died facin the enemy 'r they died a glorious death. How kin men be so lost a' ther senses?"

"But ain't this war to make people free?" Jonah asked. "Ain't we fighting to end slavery?"

"I really ain't thinkin so, Jonah," Duane answered. "I think it's more fer power n' glory. These generals ain't all got slaves an' some as don't believe in it. Some are wantin ta become governors an' sech. The leaders in the Confederacy want ther own power separ't from the leaders in Washington."

"But it's all so exciting," Jonah pursued.

"Da ya wanna kill me?" Duane asked adjusting toward the sound of his friend's voice.

"No. You're my friend," the boy answered.

"But I'm from Arkansas an one a' the enemy."

"No! You're my friend!"

"In a war, people ain't real no more. But yer right, Jonah. Yer my friend, too. I's seen friends die. Jonah, war ain't no playin! It's a Hell on earth! People, real people, are kilt! I ain't wantin it ta be yer kilt too!"

"Jonah," Captain Marshalton spoke softly, "there are many in this war that are here to save lives. I'm a doctor. I want to be a good doctor. If I hadn't offered to transfer when my sister state was seeking medical people, I'd not be here with Dee today, and there's a whole lot of new information I wouldn't have learned. But I want to learn, and have learned a lot from trying to help the wounded. These men are musicians. They offer their talents to try to take men's minds off the war. Dee's right. The fighting makes men do terrible things and things not natural to them. Some do extraordinarily brave things. Some are exceedingly kind. Give up your search for adventure on the battlefield. Find adventure in helping save lives or just enjoying being alive."

"How about some music," Zachary offered. "The band is planning to play for the regiment this evening and the others are beginning to gather."

"Yea," Jonah jumped to his feet and stretched cramped muscles. "That sounds real good."

"Give me a hand, Jonah. My feet is lost ther feelins." Duane reached his hand out as he stretched his ankles and wiggled his toes in his shoes.

Johnny joined the boy and the two pulled their friend to his feet. Pausing a moment to gain his balance, then retrieve his haversack, Duane started slowly to the tent to put his gear away. The others did the same. The fire was down to hot coals as other members of the band were emerging from their tents to gather with their comrades.

Jonah took Duane's hand to serve as his guide and they started on their way.

"You going to play with us, Johnny?" Joshua asked.

"Okay!" the youth answered. "Can I use your drum, Dee?" he asked.

"Sher by me," Duane replied.

"Be right back." Johnny dashed to the tent to get the instrument.

As soon as he returned, the three continued on to join the stream of men headed toward an open field for an evening of musical entertainment.

*   *   *

Two days later an attack was ordered on the center of the Confederate line in the belief that the movements of the previous days had left it weakened. As the division advanced, an early morning slaughter commenced from a well-fortified Confederate position and the action was called off. The following day, General Lee's army committed the same error and was repulsed. That action lasted most of the day.

The days that followed saw the II Corps moving south in the hope of drawing out the Confederate Army. But it didn't work. General Lee relocated on a whole new front, some twenty-four miles to the southeast, using the North Anna River for his line.

Jonah had returned to the supply train the morning following the band's concert. The week of activity that followed had kept him busy and out of touch with Duane's brigade. The beginning of the fourth week of May found General Birney's division engaged amidst a pelting rain, as the Federal assault attempted to drive across a bridge on the North Anna River. Following three days of action in heavy rain storms, the conflict paused for a day. At week's end the armies moved again.

As May neared its end, there was fighting further south when the armies met just north of Richmond on the Totopotomoy Creek. The Generals sidestepped from there to a tavern crossroads called Cold Harbor, and clashed once more on the final afternoon of the month.

June 1st found Hancock's Corps on the move once more. The day was oppressively hot with temperatures nearing 100 degrees. Duane and Johnny rode the wagon seat in the column of march with dust rolling all about them. Their clothes were soaked through as the sweat poured from their bodies. Its moisture attracting the dust from the air, the two were thickly covered in a sweat-splotched layer of brown.

"How much longer ya reckon this fight'll go?" the younger boy called above the grinding rattle of the wagon's wheels along the country lane. "It seems like forever," Johnny called back. "I have never seen such continuous action."

"It sher does seem as it ain't neve' gonna end," Duane complained.

"We're coming to a creek," Johnny warned. "Hang on while I run the team through."

Duane grabbed his seat tightly while his companion hollered and whipped the horses to keep them from stopping to drink the water.

"They's dyin in this heat!" Duane shouted.

"I know," Johnny agreed, "but we're ordered to keep on the move."

The column continued on across the countryside, cutting in a southeasterly direction toward the fighting which had already begun at Cold Harbor. The last to arrive, the corps finally stopped some four miles to the north of the crossroads, at the far end of the Union line. The men were quickly put to work digging fortifications. Near the end of the day, new orders came: March around the rear of the Union position to the opposite end of the line under cover of night, and be ready to attack at dawn.

Again the division moved. The oppressive heat, the dark of night, the thick dust, and a wrong turn, resulted in a slow journey which ended with exhausted troops arriving in position at about 6:30 in the morning. The attack was postponed for twenty-four hours.

Johnny pulled his wagon into position behind the brigade's segment of the defenses currently under construction. The two boys climbed into the back of the wagon bed and went to work lining up materials at the tailgate.

"They did it again," Johnny stated while he worked at the back stacking the packs and other materials as Duane felt for and passed each item.

"What's thet?" the other asked as he extended a requested item toward the voice.

"Gave Lee time to build fortifications. We won't be able to get through."

Footsteps were heard from outside as Captain Marshalton approached through the activity of the troops.

"Dee," he called, "I've a letter from your pa's company."

"Where?" the boy called excitedly, tripping over the equipment in his haste to get out of the wagon.

"The chaplain gave it to me just now. He said he's had it several days, but forgot it in all the confusion." He took the boy's hand and helped him over the tailgate and onto his feet.

"Hurry up an' read it, Dan!" The boy stood leaning against the back of the wagon.

Johnny settled on a box of medicines near the back of the wagon bed to listen to the reading of the letter. The doctor tore the end of the envelope and drew out the letter from within.

"Dear Captain," he read. "We were most excited to receive your letter and learn that Captain Kinkade's son is still alive. The captain, however, is not here. He was badly wounded in this last fighting and sent to hospital to recover. From there he is expected to be sent home. The captain believes his son is dead and I have forwarded your letter to him. Sorry I cannot give much in particulars, but I don't know where this letter may go or who may read it. I suggest, if possible, that Duane be sent home and seek his father there. Good luck, James E. Murray, Colonel, 13th Arkansas."

There was a moment of stunned silence.

"Are there any markings on the cover?" Johnny asked.

The man carefully examined the paper. "Nothing," he reported. "Only my name and unit."

"Pa's alive," Duane whispered joyously. "He's goin home!"

"When do we leave, Dan?" Johnny wondered.

"This is not the time to ask," the captain stated. "The summer campaign is just beginning. Let me see if I can think of a way to work it out. Here, Dee, put this letter in your haversack." He pushed the paper into the boy's pocket. "I'm fixing to set a pot of coffee and have a biscuit. Want to join me?"

"Yes, Sir," the boys chorused.

The three walked along the construction sites where the troops were busy digging trenches and cutting trees for their earthworks. In an open space behind an angle in the breastworks, the captain had established a temporary operating area with trestle table covered by a canvas fly. Supplies had already been placed at hand and a fire lit for coffee.

As the day wore on, the clouds thickened and the sky darkened. In the distance, there was the sound of skirmishing mixed with thunder and flashes of lightning. By late afternoon, the storm broke with heavy rain. That turned to hail and settled to a drizzle which lasted into the night.

The boys took refuge in the wagon as the soldiers along the five-mile line broke out tent halves, ponchos, or rubber gum blankets. Huddling in whatever shelter they could manage, the men passed the day reading and rereading old letters, sitting in pensive silence, or talking quietly among themselves. As night came on, some took off their coats and got out sewing kits. Each wrote his name and homeplace on a piece of paper and pinned it to his coat so that when the fight was over and his body found, his family could be told where he had died.

Night fell, but there was little sleep. Duane sat in the wagon with his friend and listened to the soft drizzle on the canvass and the quiet moaning of nearby conversations. After a while, the sounds lulled him to a drowsiness. The boy slumped against the wooden wagon bed and into dreams of reunion with his father.

*   *   *

The Confederate line extended over seven miles from the Totopotomoy Creek on the north to the Chickahominy River on the south. It consisted of a lacework of carefully constructed trenches skillfully blended into the terrain's low ridges. There was a maze of works within works, designed with a zig-zag pattern that allowed lines of fire from the side and from head on to sweep opposing lines in simultaneous action with infantry and artillery. None of this was obvious from the Union front. It had been hidden in the contours of the landscape in a countryside of field and forest and swampland.

Duane and Johnny were awakened shortly after midnight by activity along the line. Crawling from the wagon, they found the rainfall had dwindled to a thick mist and the men were busy packing their blankets and rain gear.

"Jonah's here," Johnny announced.

"What's he up ta?" Duane asked.

"He's helping to issue rations," the older youth explained.

"What da we do?" Duane wondered.

"I'm taking you to work with Dan. I'll work along the back of the line with the fellas from the band."

Johnny took his blind friend by the arm and the two worked their way along the back of the regiment. Activity was subdued as the soldiers packed their haversacks with hardtack, coffee, and sugar to last them two days, lifted their gear to their backs, and checked their weapons. A morning chill cut through the damp clothing and the swamp odors hung in the air.

"Want a cup of coffee?" the captain offered as the two arrived at his fire.

"Sher." Duane searched for his cup.

"Sounds good." Johnny untied his from its thong and held it to the spout.

"Where do you want this water, Captain?" a soldier asked, arriving with two slopping buckets.

"Put it by the tent pole," the officer directed.

The activity continued as officers talked to their companies and formed them into line of battle.

"I've got to go," Johnny said. "See you two later."

"What does it look like out there, Dan?" Duane asked as his friend departed.

"Looks quite empty, Dee," the man answered. "There's a long line of low flat hills in the distance and an empty plain between here and there."

"But ain't the other army out there?"

"Can't see them through this mist."

The misting rain ended. It was nearly time for predawn light to cut the night sky on the eastern horizon. General Birney's brigades were restless as they waited for the signal to go. All along the two-mile line occupied by Hancock's corps and two more to its right, some 50,000 infantrymen waited, poised for battle. A thin fog swirled across the fields and swamps.

"What time is it?" Duane asked.

The captain pulled his watch from its pocket. "Nearly 4:30," he replied.

Suddenly the air echoed with the lonely notes of bugles sounding the advance. The soldiers climbed from their defenses and were arranged into lines of battle, two dozen deep in places. The attack began. As two divisions of the corps stepped off, General Birney's paused to follow in support.

Duane stood by the captain, the man's hand on his shoulder, as the two listened to and watched the initial movement. Suddenly the air exploded with a concussion of sound more violent than anything the boy had experienced in all the war. Artillery thundered with volcano-like tremors far greater than the cannonade at Gettysburg. Riflery roared in scathing sheets of flame, shattering the air with a crashing fury that crushed upon the ears.

The wall of led and fire slammed into the Union front, reeling the line on impact as it spun the bodies, dead before they fell, into those of their comrades, who in turn were struck down, so that it appeared like dominoes falling, one against the other, so rapid was the slaughter. As they leaned into the fury of the hailstorm of lead, the advancing mass was so dense that there was no way for those in front to retreat, and for many behind to even fire their weapons.

The Confederate line appeared as a long cloud of smoke with flashes of artillery and musketry writhing and dancing like lightning in a storm. The roar of gunfire crescendoed across the line as the men in blue fell like cordwood, piling up all along the battle front.

Some advanced to the very edge of the Confederate works, only to be cut down by such heavy gunfire as to shred their bodies beyond recognition. The fire became so intense that every discharge of shot and shell blew apart a score of advancing soldiers sending gear and guns, and broken pieces of arms and legs and bodies exploding into the air. Within fifteen minutes, three thousand in the corps had fallen and the rest of the leading brigades were burrowing into the ground wherever they were, digging in frantically with bayonets, plates, cups, spoons, and their bare hands. At the end of an hour, the entire Union assault line was dug in.

The thunderous wave of vibration began to recede as the firepower slowed and the fiery glow along the western landscape gave way to the light of dawn in the east. An intense ringing filled the boy's ears and a creeping numbness crawled across his skin as the violent shaking of earth and air began to still.

"Is it ove'?" he asked, his own voice humming in his head.

"I'm not sure, Dee," the captain's voice was fuzzy. "It seems to be quieting, but the troops aren't returning. Even the wounded are only trickling in, a few at a time."

For the moment, the surgeon was idle. Activity in the area was slow.

"Over there!" someone directed.

Two battle-weary infantrymen assisted a wounded comrade toward the table.

"Where to, Doc?" one asked.

"Lay him here," the captain instructed.

The bloodied veteran was placed atop the table.

"How bad?" Duane asked.

"Just a minute," Dan responded as he examined the bloodied shreds of clothing and the body within.

The man was conscious, but in shock. His wide eyes peered in white contrast to the blackened face, covered with powder, smoke, and mud. Blood soaked the fabric of one trouser leg and ran from a half dozen other holes in the clothing. The two who had brought him waited momentarily for word on his condition.

"This foot is shattered and will have to come off," the doctor announced. "I won't know for a while just how serious his other wounds are. But most appear to be treatable."

"Thank you, Sir," a private said. "Take good care of him for us."

They left.

"Chloroform," Dan ordered. "I'll also need the amputation knife and saw, and two of you to steady his leg."

It was over in less than three minutes. The severed foot was tossed aside. Two men then placed the wounded man on a litter and set him aside to await an ambulance while the captain rinsed his surgical saw in a bucket of murky red water.

Throughout the morning orders were received from the commanding general for General Hancock and the other corps commanders to press the attack. The men in the field responded by pouring rapid volleys of riflery toward the enemy trenches, but none rose up to advance. There were periodic barrages of enemy artillery and riflery. The divisions in forward positions were pinned down and could neither attack nor retreat in safety. The wounded could not be reached. Enemy fire struck down any who tried. The dead could not be buried. No one was willing to call a truce to permit it.

As the sun made its journey to its zenith, the severity of the damage was gradually realized. By noon the horrifying truth was known. Nearly 7,000 Union soldiers had become casualties, most during the first fifteen minutes of devastating horror. Work at the aid stations became steady as wounded who could, crawled toward the Union works and others were brought in by some who dared to go after the fallen who seemed within their reach.

The small figure of the boy danced its way toward the operating table as Jonah weaved among the wounded who carpeted the ground and dodged the nurses and litter bearers moving among them.

"Captain Marshalton!" he cried. "Hurry! Johnny's hurt!"

"What?" the man called over the noise of commotion in the area, startled in his work by the calling of his name.

The boy worked his way to the doctor's side, ignoring the hands, wrist-deep in blood, trying to probe a man's abdomen for a bullet.

"Johnny's shot! He's needing help!" the boy cried.

"How bad?" the man asked without stopping.

"I don't know. He's trapped on the battlefield." Glistening dark eyes pleaded for help.

"I can't go!" Dan shouted in frustration and anger. "Take Dee!" His hand trembled with sudden emotion. "Oh, God!" he whispered, "bring him in safe." Turning to the boys he shouted, "Take bandages and a tourniquet!"

Jonah grabbed Duane by the shirt sleeve and began to drag him off.

"Here!" one of the nurses called and passed a pack, quickly stuffed with bandages, some stiptics, and splints.

"I cain't go fast," Duane called as he tripped over an unseen litter and fell to his knees.

"I'm sorry," Jonah cried. "I'll be more careful."

The youngster pulled his teenaged companion along the back of the Union defenses to a point where the brigade had been. Joshua met them as they arrived.

"Dee!" he exclaimed, "Zachary went out with Sammy Ellison. They're trying to crawl far enough to grab a hold of Johnny and drag him in."

"What happened?" Duane asked, worry edging his voice.

"Johnny was working with several who were helping the wounded get back to safety. They were hit by a volley of fire from the right. We know Tim Adams is dead. But others are still alive."

"They're coming in!" someone exclaimed.

A half dozen rescuers crawled back behind the defenses with four wounded in tow. They were quickly surrounded by a dozen friends who sought to render assistance.

Zachary assisted Johnny to a spot of shade under a tulip tree. Jonah dragged Duane along and the two helped settle their friend on the ground.

"Ya okay?" Duane asked as he knelt by Johnny's head.

"No," came the exhausted reply accompanied by a fit of coughing.

"You don't look bad," Jonah countered.

There was no response as the wounded youth breathed heavily, fighting for air.

"Zachary! What kin ya see?" Duane asked in a panic.

"Move aside, Jonah, and let me have a look," the man instructed.

The boy scampered backwards on his hands and feet, dragging himself to Duane's side.

"Here," Duane handed him the pack. "Hand us what we need."

The younger teen waited anxiously while the bandsman opened his friend's shirt and sought to learn his condition.

"He's shot in the lower chest," Zachary stated. "Give me your hand."

He took Duane's hand and placed it on the wound. The boy's fingers sensed the ribs and the sticky blood below the right lung. His ears picked up a soft bubbling sound as blood seeped inconsistently from the wound. The body quivered from pain and shock. Across the chest, the heart pounded frantically and Duane could feel its vibrations.

"Is he hurt enywhere else?" the youth asked.

"Grazed to the head and a hole in the flesh of his thigh," Zachary described.

"Dee," Johnny whispered. "It hurts like Hell."

"We'll git ya fixed up proper," Duane assured. "Hang in ther."

The blind teen closed his eyes in a moment of prayer and an attempt to decide what to do.

"Git a blanket," he ordered. Then to Zachary he asked, "Is the bullet still in?"

"I think not in the leg. But the one in his chest is still there."

Duane slipped his hand under his friend's back to confirm there was no exit hole. Jonah returned with the blanket.

"Thank ya, Jonah," Duane acknowledged as he used the blanket to pillow his friend's head. "He'p me ta do the bandagin, Zachary?"

"Sure," the man said.

Jonah held the pack convenient for materials while Duane gave instructions and the bandsman helped with the work. Thomas stopped by and was sent to find a litter. A stiptic was used to control the bleeding from the head wound. The leg was wrapped. After debating whether or not to probe for the bullet, it was decided to wait and the chest wound was covered. Johnny said little. His eyes pleaded for relief and he attempted at one point to help hold a bandage with his left hand. Weakness grew on the older youth and he seemed to fade in and out of sleep. Pain was obvious, but he withheld his cries and clenched his teeth on occasion.

All along the battle line, fighting continued to flare in pockets of exchanging gunfire. Supply wagons and ambulances were in continual motion. Generals, too, passed along the line to determine troop positions and levels of success.

A litter was brought and Johnny was carefully lifted onto it. The bandsmen left to carry out what assistance they could for others. Duane and Jonah remained with their wounded friend, offering him sips of water when he asked. The afternoon wore on. Jonah built a fire, found a coffee pot, and helped Duane prepare a pot of coffee. He sweetened it with some sugar from his haversack and offered sips to the wounded youth. Johnny smiled weakly in appreciation. The two young sentinels munched on hardtack to settle the grumblings in their own stomachs and shared a tin of meat from Jonah's supply.

Several of the bandsmen came and went to check on their friend's progress. Finally, as the sun was settling toward the distant horizon, Dan was able to get away. He knelt beside the boy who was like a son to him, and examined the wounds.

"Will he be okay?" Jonah asked.

Duane sat back against the tree to be out of the way. He, too, listened for the answer.

"No," the man said, emotion catching in his throat.

"Why?" Duane asked, barely audible for the tightness in his own throat.

"The bullet's still in there," he spoke with effort. "But worst, it's around his lung. He's bleeding inside and it's filling the lining around his lungs. After a while they'll collapse and he won't be able to breathe."

"Dan," Johnny tried to talk. Light coughing cut him off.

"Try to rest, Johnny," the man instructed.

"No time," the youth forced. He rested a moment before continuing. "Please . . . get . . . Dee . . . home."

"Please, Son, don't give up," the man pleaded.

"Promise . . . me," Johnny pleaded in return.

"Yes, I promise," Dan said.

"I'm not . . . quitting . . . yet." There was a moment of quiet when Johnny closed his eyes and seemed to drift away. He worked his fingers so the man knew he was still alive while he rested and caught his breath. He swallowed hard.

"Coffee?" Jonah asked.

"Yeh," the youth sighed.

The boy lifted the cooled cup of sweetened liquid to the quivering lips. Johnny sipped slowly as some leaked out and ran down the corners of his mouth. Duane crawled from the tree to get by his friend's side.

"I ain't goin home ta yer better, Johnny," he said as he felt for his friend's hand.

Their fingers met and their grip tightened.

"You've got to," Johnny said. "I'm . . . dying."

"No!" Duane shouted, then calmed himself. "Ya cain't!" he pleaded.

"I can't . . . stop . . . it," he paused, exhausted.

No one spoke for a moment. Tears slipped down Duane's cheeks. He let them go. Dan saw the grief on the boy's face and felt the inner pain of his own grief. He blinked rapidly as the moisture rose up in his own eyes and a tight pain stuck in this throat. He stood and turned away, his body shaking with silent sobbing. Jonah was lost as to what to do. At first he didn't realize it, but he, too, was crying. He wiped the tears from his eyes and sat looking on in disbelief. Death had never come this close to him before. His mother had died in childbirth and he'd never known her. He had never been really close to his father. Sure, he loved him, but it was different. It hadn't hurt to leave his father behind in a hospital, not knowing if he would ever see him again, and not caring much either. Here was a friend who was dying and he wasn't sure what that should feel like, but he did know that it would mean they could never see each other again.

"Dan," Johnny whispered, "I want . . . to go . . . home . . . to be . . . with my . . . folks."

"Oh, God, I hate this war!" the man cried. "I don't know how I can take you." The tears flowed and his voice choked. His mouth quivered with grief and his eyes searched hopelessly for an answer.

"Johnny, I love ya," Duane whispered. "Please don't die. Yer the only one I eve' had as like a brother."

Johnny's hand tightened in response. With a great effort, he lifted his left hand to place it on his younger friend's head and pulled it toward his shoulder so he could hug the sobbing boy. Duane bent beside the youth and the two embraced for a long moment.

"I love you . . . too . . . Dee." He swallowed hard and shook slightly with shallow coughing.

The embrace lost its strength and Duane gently eased his friend's arms back to his side.

"Captain Marshalton," Jonah spoke, barely audible as he worked to force his voice from an uncomfortable pain in the throat, which he'd never known before.

"What, Jonah," the man answered.

"I can take Johnny home. Me and Dee can ride with him to his folks place, then I can go with Dee to his home, too." The offer was innocently simple. There was a sense of expectation in the voice, an excitement of possible adventure.

The man smiled. "I don't think you understand, Jonah."

"Yes, I do, Sir. Johnny's going to go to sleep and he won't wake up again. But you won't have to put him in the ground. He can go with me and I'll see he gets to his own home."

Johnny smiled at the unknowing sincerity. Duane and the captain couldn't help but to laugh.

"What's wrong?" the boy asked.

"It's okay," Dan said. "You just don't quite understand what's happening here."

"Jonah . . . you're all . . . right," Johnny said. "You can . . . take me . . . home . . . anytime."

"Sher, why not," Duane asked. "We kin do it, Dan. Me an' Jonah kin do it."

"Okay by you, Johnny?" the man asked.

"Sure thing," Johnny answered. The coughing came again. "God, it hurts," he cried, the tears of pain slipping free.

Darkness came as the four had talked.

"Let's find some place more comfortable," Dan suggested.

"There's no hurry," Johnny said. "I'm okay . . . here."

Duane sent Jonah to get blankets from the wagon. He covered his friend and made his own bed beside the litter. Jonah curled up by the fire. Captain Marshalton draped his blanket over his shoulders and found an empty ammunition box to use as a seat for the night. As the boys settled to sleep, he prepared another pot of coffee, refueled the fire, and settled to keep a vigil through the night.

In the fields to the west, the wounded begged for water. Those of the living who could, slept. Others were haunted by the moaning and lay awake agonizing in their helplessness to render assistance. The sky overhead sparkled with its glittering of stars. The frogs of the river banks and swamplands filled the night with their song. The lonely man poured a cup of coffee, then sat on the box, huddled beneath his blanket, to keep watch over the dying youth. As he put the cup to his lips, a curl of steam wafted into the night air and a gentle breeze carried from the battlefield.

The smell of death was in the air.

*　　*　　*

In the hour before midnight a shadowy figure approached. The captain had drifted into a light slumber, but heard the footsteps and lifted his head.

"Captain Marshalton," the man spoke.

"What is it, Sergeant?" Dan responded.

"There's wounded coming in, Sir. Can you come and help?" The man stood waiting by the fire.

"Certainly. I'll be with you in just a minute." He stood, letting the blanket fall from his shoulders, and leaned over the youth on the litter.

Johnny's breathing was very shallow. Each breath was forced.

"Hang in there, Johnny," Dan whispered, as he gently stroked the bandaged head.

Stepping back for one last look, the captain left to attend the incoming wounded.

As dawn brightened the eastern horizon, Captain Marshalton returned to find coffee brewing and bacon sizzling. Jonah was doing the cooking under Duane's supervision. Johnny was awake and had turned his head to watch. Several of the bandsmen had come and gone. Joshua occupied the seat on the ammunition box.

"Hi," Dan greeted gently.

"Morning," the boys at the fire chorused.

Johnny forced a weak smile, but said nothing.

"He can't talk," Joshua explained as the doctor knelt by the boy's side. "There's too much pain."

"Coffee's done," Duane announced, as he carefully poured a cup for the captain.

With the cup resting on the ground, the boy hung his finger over the side and waited for it to sense the rising level of hot liquid. The coffee reached the fingertip and Duane set the pot on the ground for Jonah to take and reset in the coals of the fire.

"Here, Dan," Duane offered, holding the cup toward the captain.

"Thanks, Dee." He took the coffee, sipped some, then handed it to Joshua. "Set this on the box, please."

Unbuttoning Johnny's blood-wet shirt, Dan commented, "Let's take a look and see what's happening."

The bandage was soaked with blood which continued to seep from the wound. It bubbled up and down with every effort to breathe.

"Joshua," the captain instructed, some alarm in his tone, "pass more bandages from that pack."

The bloodied material was left in place as more was placed overtop. Once the new wrap was secured in place, the man listened carefully with his stethoscope to determine what was happening inside.

"It won't be long, Johnny," Dan stated. His voice cracked.

The youth nodded in agreement.

To the west, volleys of gunfire reminded everyone of the battle, but didn't last long.

"What's that awful stink?" Jonah asked. "They didn't kill that many horses. Did they?"

"That's the dead you're smelling, Jonah," Joshua explained. "There's acres and acres of them out there."

"People?" Jonah asked in surprise.

"Dead soldiers, rotting in the heat and sun since early yesterday." Joshua passed the cup of coffee back to the captain who had just finished closing Johnny's shirt.

"Oh." A sudden truth was realized as Jonah continued, "That's why Kyle Baker and his friends were funnin me so much every time I complained how bad the air was smelling this summer." He turned the bacon slices over on the plate, then stared at Johnny. "Do people die like animals and their bodies rot, too?"

"Thet's fer truth," Duane put in.

"Will Johnny?"

"Yes," the captain affirmed.

The boy turned his head to gaze, disbelieving, about the camp. This new reality was very upsetting.

"Jonah," Duane began, "I know's how ya feels in yer gut." The younger boy stared at the young teenager with a new respect. "It's part a' thet reality I said a'fer thet is war."

"Dee, I feel sick," Jonah cried.

"It's natural," Dan said. "It will go away."

"How's Johnny?" Joshua asked.

"The lung's give out," Dan answered. "The other one's going, too. There's a great deal of pain."

Jonah pulled the plate of bacon from the fire and set it on the ground. He wasn't hungry. Instead, he stood and walked to the captain's side to stare at Johnny. The youth forced a painful smile, then started to cough again. Blood spewed from his mouth and sprayed his clothing. Jonah turned away, confused by his feelings.

"Dee!" Johnny called hoarsely.

Duane reached toward the voice and Dan took the hand to guide him to his friend's side. The sutler's son started toward the tree, but stopped a short distance from the litter and stood watching, struck by a horrifying realization that he was witnessing death, close-up, for the first time in his life. The captain placed the blind boy's hand on that of his friend. Johnny sought to grasp the hand and affirm his friendship.

"Dan," he rasped, "give Dee my . . . things."

"I will." The tears began to flow.

Johnny began to choke and cough as blood seeped into his throat. He reached for Dan who gathered him into his embrace and held him close while the coughing continued to rack the body. Duane reached around them both and felt their last embrace, the tremors of grief, and the lost fight with death. He felt the coughing subside and the body go still. He felt the man quaking as his sobbing knew no limits and his soul was wretched to its core. Duane's tears and the pain that ripped within reached for an eternity. Suddenly the war had ended as the knowledge was born within that it was the people who had kept him from going home. Now, the one person who had been so close, was gone.

There was nothing left to live for.

But his pa was going home. Now, he too, would go home.

"Wer goin home, Johnny," he whispered. "The war's ended 'n wer goin home."

EPILOGUE

The shrill shriek of the train's whistle rent the night and intruded on the boy's dreams. A warm June breeze whipped through the open coach window, blowing across the soot-streaked face. Duane opened his sightless eyes, as he turned his head to better hear the soft snoring of his young companion, stretched across the opposite seat.

Jonah was there and he was okay.

Duane turned to let his feet slide from his bench to the floor and sat closer to the window to allow the draft to blow full upon his face, whipping his hair about his ears and stinging his forehead and cheeks with sharp twinges of pelting pinpricks. There was a fresh smell in the air of the moisture of night dew. There was a comfortable rhythm through the floorboards, through his body, of the train's clattering along the steel rails, of the engine's chugging to pull its load, of speed and motion through the countryside.

The dream had seemed so real, yet even as he lived it through his slumber, the youth kept telling himself it was only a dream. Johnny's presence at his side as he arrived in his home town of Bendton could never happen. He was dead. The box in the baggage room at the front of the coach was where he lay now.

Once more, Duane relived that last day, so long ago, and the course of events that had followed. Once more he heard Johnny's last words and shared that last embrace and felt the stillness of death. A tear slipped free as he mourned the loss of a best friend and a piece of his life. The war was only a memory. Yet it had been a way of life with some very special people for whom he cared so much. It was people who had lived and touched his life—people who were real, but were lost forever. The fighting, the battlefield, was only a detail. The people were what mattered.

"Oh, God," he thought. "They're gone—all gone." And the faces passed in his mind—Sammy Winters, the widow Katie Smith, Tod Gardner, Willis, Sergeant Raymond, Colonel Fry, Lieutenant Damien Jenkins, Jamie Wilkinson, Reverend Smyth, Thelma Dowd, Annie Hasslett, Johnny Applebee, Daniel Marshalton—the living whose lives would go on their separate ways to never meet again and the dead who could never again be more than a distant memory.

After Johnny's death, while the battlefield continued to echo with cannonades and rifle volleys, Dan had taken the body to his surgery table. There, with Duane's assistance, he had cut an artery in the leg and pumped a chemical solution through the corpse, forcing out the body's blood. It was called embalming, the captain had explained. It preserved the body so that it wouldn't decay. A casket was fashioned from the boards of a damaged out-building.

Johnny's body was bathed and dressed in his own uniform, then gently laid in the box which had been lined with a blanket spread over a bed of straw. Before the lid was nailed in place, Dan and Duane bade their friend farewell. Sitting by the open window of the railway coach racing through the night, the boy brushed his fingertip across his lips as he remembered again the last kiss. He had felt the stilled face with his hands and had bent over the simple wooden edge of the casket to kiss the forehead. Its smooth solid coldness that was like polished marble was impressed forever in Duane's memory, along with the sound, a moment later, of the pounding hammer as Dan drove the nails into the wooden box.

For two more days the volleys and cannonades had roared back and forth between the armies. It was Tuesday before the first burial parties could set about to attend the dead. By then, only two of the thousands who had fallen remained alive to receive care for their wounds. The rest of the week had been quiet as the two armies set about the grim task of burying the corpses. The remains had decomposed badly in the heat of the June sun. None were more than rotted flesh clinging to partially exposed bones and grinning teeth where lips had been, bound together by ragged uniforms. They were heaped upon wheelbarrows and wagons to be carted to large excavations for common graves. There, these nameless thousands were dumped and covered over with the dirt of the battlefield. Some found a final resting place in a shell hole, others in a trench which was closed over them where they lay.

It was during these days of quiet that Duane had begun his journey homeward. The captain had arranged for the use of an ambulance to transport Duane, Jonah, and Johnny to the Virginia Central Railroad near Hanover Court House. There he had seen them safely onto the train and had given last instructions on how to transfer trains as they worked their way west from railroad to railroad. All had been written out on paper and given to Jonah, along with all Duane's army pay which the captain had saved over the years, to keep in his pocket for reference and to pay expenses along the way. Duane knew then that he'd never see Captain Marshalton again. The two said their good-byes, Duane speaking to his friend through the open window of the coach as the train eased out of the station.

It had been a long and lonely trip, first to Gordonville where the small party transferred trains to the Orange and Alexandria Railroad, then on into eastern Tennessee and points north. Jonah was good company and very clever when the need arose, to talk his way through uncertainty or seek information or get the best price on food or refreshment. He was dependable as he made it his business to be sure Johnny's casket was carefully moved from car to car as they transferred trains, and that a trunk, carrying their combined belongings, passed with the wooden box. Jonah kept his rifle with him, tied in a blanket to avoid questions. Duane kept his drum, with its strap attached, to rest at his feet or be carried slung over a shoulder.

Somewhere in the middle of farm country, the train slowed as it approached a small station where a single lantern cast a feeble glow across a wooden platform occupied by a solitary figure.

The engine's whistle announced its arrival and its bell clanged mournfully in the night as the brakes screeched, steel against steel, in a gathering chorus of brakemen on the various cars turning down their wheels to check the forward movement and assist the engine's efforts to halt the train. Finally, the entire consist came to a clattering stop and a quiet of sorts settled about the air as Duane listened to the hissing steam in the locomotive's piston chambers and the quiet conversation of the engineer and the station agent. Their voices were clear on the night air as information was passed of an eastbound freight train, due to pass within the half hour. To either end of the train, switches were thrown, their metallic slap, swift and sudden. The passing track was open. For now, it was a time of waiting and stilled silence.

An eerie quiet enveloped the scene as the absence of noise and motion allowed for a moment of peace. Jonah stirred, but did not waken. Duane opened his grey jacket as the stilled air grew warm, then settled comfortably to drift back to sleep.

Suddenly, a distant whistle cut the night. It wailed in gathering intensity, racing eastward, ever closer in the night. It quickly crescendoed, was upon the pass track with a sudden whoosh of air pressure clattering noisily by in thunderous smoke and soot, then passing behind and beyond to fade as quickly back into the night. Once more the switches clapped as they were realigned.

"Board!" a single voice called from the station platform. There were two short blasts on the whistle. A surge of steam accompanied the squealing turning of the brake wheels. The train strained and clattered into motion. The station slipped slowly out of view.

An hour later, Duane felt the warmth of the new day's sunrise as the first strong beams of sunlight struck out across the land and caressed his face through the open window. In his mind he saw the light playing in the soft blond curls of Johnny's hair as he lay silently on the litter that last morning of his life. He saw Jamie on his litter in the wilderness as they spoke of the friends from another year. He felt a song he'd sung with his companions in Company K. Quietly the words stole into his mind. Softly he sung them in the privacy of his imagination, the words barely audible in the early light of morning amidst the clatter of the coach's wheels.

Into the ward of the clean white-wash'd halls,
Where the dead slept and the dying lay;
Wounded by bayonets, sabres, and balls,
Somebody's darling was borne one day.
Somebody's darling, so young and so brave,
Wearing still on his sweet, yet pale face—
Soon to be hid in the dust of the grave,
The lingering light of his boyhood's grace.
Somebody's darling, somebody's pride,
Who'll tell his mother where her boy died?

Give him a kiss but for somebody's sake,
Murmur a prayer for him soft and low;
One little curl from its golden mates take,
Somebody's pride it was once you know;
Somebody's warm hand has oft rested there,
Was it a mother's, so soft and white?
Or have the lips of a sister so fair,
Ever been bathed in their waves of light?
Somebody's darling, somebody's pride,
Who'll tell his mother where her boy died?

The song drifted off and a feeling of melancholy held the boy in his reverie of sad memories.

"Dee," Jonah's voice startled him from his thoughts. "Will Johnny go to heaven? Will he be with God?"

The voice and the question caught the youth completely by surprise.

"I ain't knowin fer sher, Jonah." Duane pulled himself from his dreams and reflections. "He sher oughtta."

Jonah had been wakened by his companion's song and had listened without moving until it was over. Now he stretched, sat up, and moved to the window to gaze at the passing countryside, washed in the radiant glow of the dawning day.

"Is God really there?" he asked without turning from the window.

"He has ta be, Jonah." Duane faced the small voice. "We ain't no accident. The flowers 'n trees 'n living creatures ya's lookin at ain't no accident neither."

"How'd you know what I was seein?"

"What else would ya be seein?"

The two smiled at each other.

"Is Johnny with God?" Jonah asked.

"He sher is, Jonah," Duane replied. "An' he's with us, too. As long as we ain't fergittin ar time tageth'r, he ain't neve' goin from us."

"What about the box?"

"He's ther, too. But he's in thet trunk as has his thin's. An when his box is in the ground, his thin's 'll still be with me, an' so will he."

Somewhere else in the car a child whined. A voice soothed. Others in the car awakened to the new day as the quiet was gradually invaded by renewed conversations, arguments, card games, and the telling of wonderments. Some stood to stretch or pace the aisle. Duane and Jonah paused to listen. The car door from the baggage room opened and the conductor entered.

"Vincennes, next stop," he announced. "We stop for breakfast and connections north and south." He strode through the car to pass his announcements to the passengers on the cars behind.

"That's a blessing," Jonah stated.

"What is?" Duane asked.

"I'm starvin!" the boy smiled.

"Yeh, me too," Duane agreed. "What da we do here fer changin trains?"

Jonah took the information packet from his pocket. "Here we get a train for Terre Haute. But we gotta wait a couple hours and they serve breakfast."

"Sounds fine by me." Duane stretched and resettled himself in his seat.

The engine's whistle announced the approaching stop and the train began to slow.

* * *

At Vincennes, Jonah supervised the transfer of the wooden casket and the trunk to a baggage cart for loading on the northbound train to Terre Haute. Once in place by the tracks of the Evansville and Crawfordsville Railroad, the boys left the train of the Ohio and Mississippi Railroad to enjoy breakfast while the locomotive's crew went about the business of taking on wood and water. After a brief flurry of activity following a one-hour breakfast layover, the train continued on its way. The two boys settled on a station bench to await their next train.

By mid-morning they were on their way again. At Terre Haute, Indiana, they stayed the night to change trains again as the pair continued west the following morning on the St. Louis, Alton, and Terre Haute Railroad. By noon they had crossed into Illinois and arrived at their final stop in Paris. There, an elderly Doctor Jamison Clancy met them at the station, loaded the trunk and Johnny's casket onto a buckboard, and took the two on the final leg of Johnny's journey, north to the farming town of Cedar Knoll.

* * *

The flatbed wagon, drawn by a pair of chestnut mares, bounced along the lonely dirt lane that was the road north. The flat landscape of grasslands and fields stretched away from the roadway across the monotony of the Central Plains toward distant horizons. The air was warm and quiet, yet blended with the sounds of insects, chattering in hordes so as to sound as one constant wave of noise, rising and falling across the open country. Duane rode on the bouncing spring-board bench, to the right of the veteran doctor.

Jonah sat behind, perched on the front edge of the casket, with his hands gripping tightly on the iron rail seatback, to maintain his balance for the rough ride.

Doc Clancy was a paunchy sixty-seven years of hard, country experience. His white hair flowed in thick waves which hung just above his collar and was kept neatly trimmed. Clean-shaven, his face was lined with comfortable crinkles which reflected wisdom, humor, and a firmness that was not to be questioned. His ever-present brown leather medical bag rode securely on the floor, just beneath the seat. Firm hands held the reins. Yet there was a gentleness in their pull so that the horses were not in pain from the bit of the bridle, though they were never in question as to their driver's intentions.

The loneliness of the ride from the station had been filled with conversation along the way and an occasional greeting from a close-by farmhouse.

"You'd have really liked the Applebees," Doc was saying. "They were a good, God-fearing couple who were filled with love for their neighbors as well as their son. It was truly unfortunate that sickness took them both. Before the war, Mr. Marshalton had become so well-known as a caring and compassionate doctor that the community was most happy when he took Johnny as his adopted son. We knew we were in for three generations of really good doctorin. Now the war has ended that. Johnny is dead and Doctor Marshalton is gone. We hope he'll return when the fightin's done. And we can't wait for it to end."

"Yer people ta holdin strong feelin's 'gainst us Rebs?" Duane asked.

"I'm afraid there's some as will give you a darn hard time, Dee. But there's others that have a way of letting a body make his own way of his own merits." The man glanced at the youth beside him and smiled with the satisfaction that he had rightfully judged the teenager as a young man of fine character.

"Do they kill Rebs in Cedar Knoll?" Jonah asked. "'Cause Dee's my friend and I'll hurt anyone who hurts him. I got a musket and

Dee can still use a gun real good." The boy's voice was resolute with loyalty and a firm belief in his and Duane's ability to fend for each other.

"I ain't knowin I kin still shoot good," Duane declared. "And I ain't neve' know'd ya ta hurt a fly, Jonah. Please don't say nothin thet'll git ya hurt none."

"I really don't think there's anything that serious about to happen in Cedar Knoll," Doc Clancy assured. "We're going to put you up with Charlotte Ross. She's the president of the Ladies' Auxiliary of the church and will see to your needs while you're with us. She's also a sort of matriarch for the town, being its oldest citizen at ninety-four years, and still very spry and alert. Her hearing's gone some and she's blind without her glasses. But trust me, she's a very able lady and you will have the best she and our community can offer."

"Why fer da ya say thet?" Duane asked.

"Johnny's our darling. And you being such a friend of his makes you very special, too."

"But ya all ain't knowin much a me an' Johnny's life tageth'r. We's been off ta the war an all."

"Daniel Marshalton sent us a telegram while you've been journeying across the country to bring our Johnny home. He said a lot of real proud things about you and told us some of Jonah, too."

"What did he say about me?" the boy asked.

"He said most how you were Duane's eyes and were responsible for taking care of all the information for you both as you traveled."

"Oh," Jonah smiled. "Does that mean I'm important?"

"Very important," Doc affirmed.

"Ya sher is," Duane agreed.

"You want to hear about me and the war?" Jonah asked.

"I'd be honored," the man said.

For the next half hour the older two listened while Jonah entertained them with the story of his life as a sutler's boy. His ramblings were surely not boring and often quite humorous. Eventually, the outlying farms around Cedar Knoll appeared and the journey neared its end.

Duane sensed the town's nearness. There was a change in the air as a noise level of activity and the presence of people invaded the quiet that had been, and the clatter of the wagon was echoed off nearby structures. A dog's bark and the cackle of chickens busily pecking about a farmyard gave evidence to an approaching community.

"Is this Cedar Knoll?" Duane asked, when Jonah paused in his account.

"Sure is," the doctor confirmed. "There's a small business district of shops, bank, sheriff, cafe, hotel, feed store, and the like. A school house and church are on the northeast edge of this district. The side streets are mostly homes and some trades such as the shoemaker and cabinetmaker. The cemetery is north of town about a quarter mile out."

As the wagon's clatter blended with the traffic on Main Street, its passengers were absorbed into the routine of activity. Few acknowledged its arrival, yet many took note of the newly-arrived visitors, caked with the dust of the road, accumulated over the miles of travel from the rail stop at Paris.

"Where d' we go fi'st?" Duane asked.

"We'll stop at my house where you can get cleaned up. Then we'll go to the hotel for dinner and on to Mrs. Ross's place." The man guided his team across the opposite lane of the dusty street and onto a side street, somewhat smaller, but just as dusty.

"What about Johnny?" Jonah asked.

"We're cutting down Murray's Alley, here, to the back of the undertaker's shop. Mr. Bernard knows we're stopping and will take good care of Johnny until the burial this Saturday."

A tall thin, sad-faced man in his fifties, Jethro Bernard helped unload the wooden casket and carry it into the workroom in the back of his shop. There it was placed on two wooden horses to await his further attention. He bade the trio good-bye and closed the door without any further visiting.

The wagon continued to the end of the alley where it turned away from the center of town and crossed over to a tree-lined lane named Fox Street. A wooden walk followed either side and was edged with clean wooden houses with roofed porches across their fronts and gingerbread trim along their roof-lines and eves. The vehicle turned in at a light tan dwelling trimmed in a burnt orange color.

"This is it," Clancy announced.

Stopping at a small side porch, the trunk was unloaded by the path to the step, then the team and wagon put into the carriage barn. Water was drawn from the pump by the back door and grain was dippered from a feed bag into the mangers. The horses were content. The man led the boys back to the house where they could bathe in the backyard tub and put on a clean change of clothes.

$$* \quad * \quad *$$

The two days before the funeral passed quietly. Charlotte Ross proved to be a woman with a golden heart. But first appearance had raised serious doubts. She was a spindly old grey-haired lady, wrinkled as a prune, with legs like broom sticks and long bony fingers which looked fragile as egg shell. The boys quickly learned she had a gritty strength as she took them shopping for new clothes and managed to move from store to store and around within each, with such ease and speed as to leave them both exhausted.

In the afternoon she took them to help with chores as she fed the chickens, gathered eggs, worked her garden, and milked her cow. They helped prepare and clear the meals. In the evening they sat with her on the porch, in one of the four red wooden rocking chairs that graced the house, and shared their stories about Johnny and Dan. They were well known to her and she craved every detail of their lives in the war. Duane soon learned there was a part of each he'd never before known as the grand old lady spun tales of life around Cedar Knoll and some of the childhood pranks each had played. It was hard to think of them as boys of ten or twelve, but Charlotte Ross had known them then, and the things each had done were embarrassing, daring, and endearing in turn.

Friday evening after the supper dishes had been put away, Duane and Jonah joined Mrs. Ross on the back porch where each in turn perched upon a high stool while she painstakingly trimmed his hair. The late sunlight of the June evening was helpful to her failing eyesight and cooler with the evening breeze. While the sun's lengthening rays continued to stray through the bedroom windows on the southwest side of the house, the three adjourned to the room the boys shared to sort through the freshly laundered clothes which the woman had laid across the bed earlier in the afternoon. She had already inspected and repaired those items which had been worn through or torn. Now, Jonah picked out his Union uniform clothing while Duane advised Mrs. Ross in the selection of his uniform items. They looked very neat all washed and sewn. The woman felt proud as she envisioned the boys, dressed smartly in their clean clothes.

Duane asked that his field gear be taken from the trunk so he could be sure that it was clean and polished. Jonah wanted his gear, too. Pack, blankets, rain gear, mess gear, tent half—all these items were carefully returned to the trunk. Belt, canteen, cap box, cartridge pouch, revolver, bayonet, rifle, haversack—all were to be clean to be worn for the funeral. Drum and sticks would also be worn. For Johnny there would be one last long roll.

Everything was in readiness. The trunk lid was closed and the uniforms laid neatly across its rounded top. The drum and accoutrements were gathered neatly on the floor beside it. Satisfied that all was in proper readiness, the old lady and her charges went out on the front porch to watch the sun go down and the June bugs flicker in the gathering darkness.

The early morning sun shown brightly outside. A warmth flooded the bedroom, but was absent of the strong rays of the rising sun since the room's windows were on the shadow side of the house. Still, Duane could sense the light as the crowing cock and twittering sparrows invaded his subconsciousness and brought him fully awake. The sizzling aroma of pan-fried ham blessed his nose and aroused an appetite. The smell of coffee and baking biscuits added to the delicious smell of morning.

"Jonah," Duane called softly, "ya 'wake?"

There was no answer.

"Jonah?"

Duane flung his arm out to waken the youngster who slept at his side. But the covers were empty.

"Thet little sneak," he thought. "He's already at the food."

Throwing the covers aside, the boy sat up and crawled to the foot of his bed and searched for his trousers on the top of the trunk. Finding the piled clothing, he quickly dressed, added his socks and shoes, then stood to orient himself. Carefully Duane worked his way around the bed and across to the door. Trusting in part a mental image of the lay of the house, he found his way from the bedroom to the kitchen. He paused in the kitchen doorway.

"Mornin, Dee," Jonah greeted.

"Good morning," Charlotte's cracked high voice joined. "Are you hungry?" she asked.

"I sher is, Ma'am," the youth stated. "An the fixin's sher do smell handsome."

"Come on," Jonah encouraged. "I'm standin at your chair and it's clear from where you stand."

Guided by the voice, Duane approached the table, felt for the chair, and eased himself into the seat.

"Put a cup of coffee for Dee. Would you please, Jonah?" the aged voice quavered.

"Yes, Ma'am," Jonah responded.

"Breakfast 'll be along shortly," the woman stated.

Duane sipped the coffee while he waited, listening all the while to the bustle of the kitchen activity and savoring its perfumed air of wood smoke and food.

"It sher ain't been natural these couple weeks," the youth remarked. "The war's so fer off an' ain't likely ta eve' be near agin. Yet it's bin sech a reg'lar part a ma days."

"Our lives change," Mrs. Ross comforted. "Chapters end and are closed forever as new ones begin and take their place. But they stay forever a part of us, tucked away in our memories. Like a dream, they drift with our past, and with them sometimes go some very important people who touched our lives, will last with those memories forever, but will never cross our lives again."

She paused to gaze about the kitchen, her own mind flooded with the memories of nearly a century past. Her hands held a plate of eggs and ham which began to quiver as it was forgotten with reflections on another time.

"Do you want me to put that on the table?" Jonah asked.

"Wha? Oh, sure, Jonah. Thank you." She handed the plate to the boy who set it in the middle of the table.

"The war's like thet," Duane thought aloud. "An' when I git home, it'll mean ta start a differ'nt life. I ain't knowin fer sher as it'll be. But ain't nothin, nohow, gonna eve' be the same agin. It's like ma whole life is gone an' now it's all . . . it's all . . . jest differ'nt."

"I really do know how you feel, Dee," Charlotte assured as she brought a plate of biscuits to the table. "My life has stretched a very long time. I was born before this land was ever settled. I was just a child when General Washington fought the British and have seen this country grow from its very beginning." She sat in her chair at the end of the table and motioned for Jonah to be seated, too. "My life has seen many chapters open and close. It is very hard. But we do it. And the past falls away so fast that it seems it never happened, but truly was just a dream."

The aged voice of wisdom had scratched unstable on the boy's ear, but the message had penetrated to his soul and he felt it deeply for the truth he knew it was.

Breakfast was consumed in a short time with little conversation. The boys did the dishes as the elderly matriarch inspected their work and put each piece in its proper place.

Returning to the bedroom at Jonah's hand, Duane put on his gunbelt and the rest of his gear as Jonah did the same. The revolver had been Johnny's. The captain had acquired it to replace the musket long before they'd transferred to the east. It was loaded and ready for use, yet Duane had never known his friend to need it. Spare cylinders were in the cartridge pouch, ready should the need arise. Johnny's haversack and personal things were left in the trunk. As Duane slipped his own over his head and adjusted it at his side, he slipped his hand inside and wrapped his fingers around Jamie's cap box. It was reassuring to feel its presence and to know the map was folded within. After a moment's reflection on the war he'd left behind, the youth quickly finished preparations as he reached for his hat, and finally, his drum.

Jonah had his own gear, including the rifle which rested against the trunk. His belt held a bayonet as well as cap box and cartridge box. He flopped his forage cap with its II Corps clover pin upon his head, took up the rifle, and was ready to go.

"Ya ready?" Duane asked.

"Yeh. Are you,?" Jonah replied.

"I'm ready," Duane confirmed.

"Here's your stick," Jonah offered, taking it from where it rested across a chair. "Give me your arm and I'll guide you to the door. You can help hitch the widow's rig and we can go."

"Lead on," Duane instructed as he reached out his hand. "But ya best be careful as I ain't fer runnin inta thin's."

"Okay," the youngster smiled.

They headed for the bedroom door.

*   *   *

The two and a half days that Duane had spent at the Ross farmhouse had not prepared him for the event that unfolded Saturday morning. He never dreamed that anyone other than he had grieved over Johnny's death. Three hundred and seventeen people gathered for the funeral—the entire community. Old Doc Clancy had seen to it ahead of time that no one would visit at Charlotte's farm until after the services.

Johnny's casket had been placed on a black-draped frame in the front of the church. It had been there since the night before, covered with the flag that usually hung at the schoolhouse. The people had come to pay their respects, filing past the box since the previous night. Some of his boyhood friends had spent the night in the church pews, to sit with him one last time.

There were the regular church-goers of the congregation and those who had never attended. The building was packed with people crowded into its pews and standing all about the walls and in the aisles. More than a hundred who couldn't fit inside, stood outside the open doors.

When Charlotte Ross's rig pulled up, a quiet settled on the crowd.

"Oh, God!" Jonah whispered under his breath.

"What?" Duane asked.

"There's hundreds of folks here, Dee. Is this right, Mrs. Ross?" A very humble Jonah turned sheepishly to the woman.

"It's right, Jonah," she whispered, loud enough for both boys to hear. "Everyone who knew Johnny has come to say good-bye. Some have even brought their young-uns who have no idea what this is about."

The three stepped down from the buggy to be met by old Doc Clancy in his finest white shirt and dark suit. He escorted the party into the church and down the aisle to the front. The doctor walked with Mrs. Ross and Duane with Jonah. The people pushed aside just enough to let them pass, then closed upon the open

110

space as soon as the four had moved ahead. The boys suddenly felt self-conscious with the drum and rifle in tow. But there was nothing else to do but carry them along.

A hushed gathering watched, their sniffling and stifled sobs intruding intermittently upon the quiet. The four approached the sanctuary. Duane reached out to touch the box, to be sure it was the same, and found its feel to be the wood that had been taken from the field of battle.

"It has a flag," Jonah whispered. Then, as everyone watched, he laid the rifle across the top.

Duane sensed that something had happened because he felt the movement when Jonah let go of his hand.

"What?" he asked.

"I put the gun on the casket," the boy explained.

Duane knew what to do with the drum. He set it on the floor in front of the black fabric. As a sudden afterthought, he reached into his haversack. His fingers touched the cap box, but slipped aside in search of a roll of bandaging cloth which he carried of habit. Withdrawing his hand, he placed the roll beside the rifle. Doc Clancy struggled to keep from crying out loud. He knew the meaning of the fabric. He guided his party to four chairs which had been placed for them beside the casket.

The service went on with prayers and words and music from the town's band and the church's choir. To Duane it was but a confusion of noise which wandered in his head, as he sat suffering the heat and the close stuffy air that smelled of sweaty bodies packed tightly inside the small church. He was a stranger in this company. He just wanted to be alone with Johnny. Couldn't anyone understand?

A group of local youths carried the wooden box from the church the quarter mile to the graveyard. Jonah recovered his rifle and Duane his drum and bandage roll. The flag was folded and left behind to be returned to the schoolmaster later.

The procession was a surging wave of humanity as the gathering walked to the open grave site. There, Duane bid a final farewell as he played the long roll one final time. Some words were said.

Many tears were shed. The box was lowered by rope into the open hole and the dirt shoveled in echoing with a hollow sound as the first clumps bounced off the wood. A thin slab of oak had already been carved:

John Davidson Applebee
born February 23, 1848
died June 4, 1864

There was no more. Beside him were the graves of his parents. Here the family slept together, gathered in eternity.

Returning home with Mrs. Ross, Duane and Jonah found themselves swamped with visitors throughout the balance of the day. Most came out of curiosity. A few stopped out of genuine concern, knowing Johnny as they did and realizing the friendship he must have shared with Duane.

The boys were drained emotionally. For Jonah it was another look at the reality of life and the finality of death. He was emotionally numbed.

Duane and Jonah slept soundly that night, passed a quiet Sunday, then departed with the doctor on Monday to ride south again to Paris where they would take the train once more to continue the journey to Duane's home in Bendton, Arkansas. Once aboard the train, Duane felt the final passing of that part of his life that had been the war. There was no box aboard this train. It was left behind, secure in the ground; its occupant asleep beneath the sod, covered by the dust of the grave. The chapter was closed, forever.

*   *   *

The afternoon sun beat hot on the wooden decking of the wharf. Overhead a blue, cloudless sky was busy with crows and pigeons who scavenged noisily for any refuse or food, abandoned on land or water. Black laborers unloaded wagons and muscled bales of cotton and other cargoes to align them for loading on riverboat or barge. Napoleon, Arkansas, was a busy port of junction where the Arkansas River emptied into the wide open expanse of the great Mississippi.

It was July as Duane and Jonah wandered out onto the busy decking to await the arrival of the **Queen**. Their journey had taken them by rail to St. Louis, then by riverboat to Napoleon, a distance of more than 600 miles. It had taken eight days and an extra two of waiting in Napoleon. **Ozark Queen** was the next boat scheduled to stop at Napoleon on its way up the Arkansas River.

Walking slowly to allow Duane to guide on his younger friend's voice, the two carried their trunk between them. Jonah also carried the rifle, wrapped and tied in its blanket; and Duane carried his drum which hung from the strap across his shoulder. Each wore the lightest elements of his uniform. Jackets and vests were in the trunk along with all else except haversack and canteen.

"Stop!" Jonah whispered loudly. "They're movin cotton bales."

The pair paused until Jonah gave the all clear, then continued on until Jonah figured they were in a good location.

"Let's put it here," he suggested.

The trunk was lowered to the flooring and both settled comfortably on its lid. The drum hung low enough to rest on the plank decking.

"What time ya reckon it is?" Duane asked.

Jonah scanned the sky. "I'd guess about three o'clock," he answered.

"The man ta the ticket winda' said as it was due near ta four. Should be hearin her soon." The thirteen-year-old turned so the smell of the water suggested he was facing the river. "How much money we got yet, Jonah?" he asked.

"After the tickets, about sixty-three dollars."

The noise of activity played on Duane's mind and he tried to remember how it looked. He asked Jonah to describe what was happening and the younger boy was eager to respond. Eventually his chatter was interrupted by the distant sounds of a steam whistle.

"Thet's her," Duane announced. "I r'memb'r the tone of her whistle."

"I can see her smoke," Jonah stated.

"When she puts in, Jonah, I'll wait here an ya go find the captain. His name is Kearny."

"Okay," the boy agreed. He stood and leaned the rifle against the trunk. "I want to look around."

"Jest don't git lost," Duane advised.

"I won't," the other promised.

As the minutes passed, activity picked up with the approach of the boat. So, too, did a sense of excitement in the air. The wild screams of local boys signaled the challenge of races to the incoming vessel. Duane heard the splashes as several dove into the river to swim out toward the **Queen**.

"Look's like fun," Jonah said, returning from a short exploration of the activity in the area.

"Ya ain't even thinkin a goin with 'em," Duane commanded.

"Don't know as I can swim that far," Jonah assured. "Besides, I thought you might like this. I got it from a farmer over a ways in the crowd."

"What is it?" He held out his hand for the offering.

"It's a honey comb and a loaf of bread."

The treasures were placed in the open hands.

"Wrap 'em an' stow 'em in yer have'sack. Captain Kearney'll have some coffee an we kin eat this tanight."

"Sure. That sounds like a good idea."

The bread and honey were put away for later. A surge of commotion and the sound of smoke rolling from the stacks as the wheel slowed against the water, confirmed that the riverboat was on the verge of tying up. Winches squeaked, orders were shouted above the noise of massed passenger conversations. The boat bumped against the edge of the wharf as the linesmen tossed the ropes to waiting hands which quickly wrapped them on the heavy cleats to hold the vessel fast against the wooden platform. The gangways were lowered. A sudden surge of movement burst forth as people rushed to disembark and laborers began to move freight, cargo, and luggage.

"Kin ya see the ship's captain?" Duane asked.

"He's at the upper railing shouting at people on the deck."

"Try ta git ta him an tell him I'm here."

"You think he'll remember you?"

"He did a time back. I'm sher he will now."

"Okay. I'll be back in a bit."

Jonah danced his way through the crowd, cavorting to one side or the other of a burdened worker or departing passenger. At one point, a pile of luggage was in his way and he vaulted across. Bouncing onward against the tide of movement, he soon worked his way to the gangway and across its edge to the vessel's deck. Dashing up the broad risers of the grand staircase, he was soon climbing the side stairs to the upper deck near the wheelhouse.

"Hey, Boy!" an angered captain barked. "Stop where ya are. Ya ain't allowed up here!"

"Are you Captain Kearny?" Jonah asked.

"Who be wantin ta know?" the blue-clad man shot back.

"Dee, I mean Duane Kinkade. He sent me to find the captain."

"Who!" the man exclaimed. "Dee's alive!?" He turned to meet the boy on the steps. "Is he here?"

"Yes, Sir," Jonah pointed. "He's sittin out there on the trunk with the drum beside him."

"He's changed," the man stated as he saw the youth in the distance. "There's a strange look ta him."

"He's blind, Captain Kearny. I came with him to be his eyes."

The man suddenly paused to study the dark-haired youngster he had bellowed at a moment before. A spirited bit of a boy, he thought, then smiled. "You'll do all right, Boy. What's yer name?"

"Jonah Christopher, Sir." He looked the captain over from head to toe, sizing him up and deciding he could be trusted. A tenseness slipped away and the boy felt relaxed within.

"Well, Jonah. Ya kin see as I'm busy. Ya git thet friend a yers on board quick an bring him ta the wheelhouse. Ya kin leave yer thin's ta the top a' the grand staircase."

"Yes, Sir, Captain."

The boy disappeared as quickly as he had come and William Kearny watched as he bounced off toward his friend, then gently helped him to gather their gear and walk toward the boat. The slender figure in the tailored blue captain's uniform reached into a pocket for his pipe and tobacco. As he watched the activity below, he knocked the ash from the bowl into his palm, dumped it on the breeze, and proceeded to refill it from the pouch. By the time the bowl was packed and the match was struck for the light, he heard the footsteps on the stair treads. He turned to meet the boys.

"Howdy, Dee," he greeted as the two reached the top of the step.

"Hi," Duane returned, extending his hand.

Jonah stepped aside, placing his friend's hand on the railing for reference.

"It sher is good ta see as yer alive," the man said.

"Is my pa alive?" Duane asked. "Da ya know if'n he's headed ta home?"

"Yes, Dee. He's gone home." The man released his grip of Duane's hand and put both hands on the youth's shoulders. "Let me look ya ov'r." He studied the figure before him. "Ya sher have done a heap a growin. I kin see, too, it's bin a hard couple a years."

"Yes, Sir," Duane responded. "I sher am glad ta see ya, Captain. I cain't wait ta be back home."

"Ya hungry?"

"Sher is."

"Well ya both come with me. You, too, Jonah," he repeated as the boy hesitated. "We'll put ya in a fi'st class cabin where ya kin leave yer gear an' head on down to the dinin saloon an git a fi'st class meal."

He reached for Jonah's shoulder to motion him by to guide Duane back down to the passenger deck. As the two boys descended the steps, Kearny paused to draw on his pipe and to observe the care with which Jonah guided his blind friend, yet tried to hold back and allow Duane his own lead whenever possible.

The boys were settled in a very comfortable cabin. Their gear moved in, they went with the captain to dine at his table in the nearly empty saloon. The evening was spent settled in deck chairs outside the captain's cabin, deep in conversation while each shared his news of the war and told of his experiences. Coffee was brought from the galley and the bread and honey shared around. Finally all retired for the night.

Ozark Queen laid over until morning while laborers worked to stack the wood racks full of fuel and to pile extra on the deck outside the engine room so that the sternwheeler would be ready for a straight run up-river. The journey was expected to take three days if the weather cooperated and stops went as planned and were kept brief.

In the days that followed, the boys took their ease, lounging on deck chairs, watching the activity in the grand saloon, visiting the wheelhouse, leaning on the rail to watch the landscape slide by. It was a lazy time, a comfortable time, a time where everything beyond the world of the vessel itself was temporarily forgotten. The boat was in and out of several ports of call along the way. Otherwise, the rhythm of the engine, its great piston rods and drive bars, the swoosh of the billowing smoke, the continuous splash of the wheel—all ran constant, day and night, their all-present motion surging through every fiber of the riverboat. One last time the boys sat together on the grand staircase as the river went to night with the last glow of day fading to velvet black on the western rim of the water.

Finally, in the early morning of the fourth day, as the sun hung low casting long shadows across the water, the river town of Ozark came into view. In the midst of the gathered passengers and their varied conversations, Jonah stood with Duane at the forward railing of the passenger deck and described the approach. Captain Kearny joined the two for just a moment to assure them he would see them ashore and help secure transportation to Bendton. Then he was gone to attend the business of bringing his vessel into port.

The dawning day continued to brighten as the sun climbed higher in the east. Within his mind and body, Duane sensed another dawn—of excited anticipation. Before this day was ended, he would be home. A tingling ran his spine and his body trembled with the sensation. Jonah sensed the excitement in the hand that gripped the railing beside his. He saw the white in the knuckles and the slight tremor in the wrists.

For Jonah the feeling was different. Deep inside a sense of apprehension was born. What would become of him once Duane was home? No longer would there be a need for the younger companion who had been his eyes, his caring guide who navigated the journey over 1800 miles. As a tingling of anticipation rose within the thirteen-year-old youth, a tear escaped to slip down the cheek of the ten-year-old sutler's boy.

The **Queen**'s whistle sang on the morning air to announce her arrival. As the wharf slipped closer, linesmen prepared to tie her in and deck hands stood by to lower the gangways. The rhythm of the engines slowed. Activity stilled, awaiting the moment of contact. Gliding gently on the water, the vessel bumped against the pilings. A sudden burst of commotion followed as people and goods moved between the riverboat and the wharf.

*　　*　　*

Following breakfast aboard the sternwheeler, Captain Kearny had the boy's belongings moved to the Kolstee Freight Company's offices while he took Duane and Jonah to arrange for their passage to Bendton on the morning freight run. Nathaniel Kolstee saw to it that their gear was added to the day's shipment and the boys were put in the care of the driver to ride with him on his delivery run to the freight house at Bendton. By eight o'clock in the morning, they were on their way once again.

There was a flurry of conversation at the start of the trip as the driver answered some questions about changes in the past two years. But he seemed a tight-lipped and reserved man in his thirties, allowing them to know him only as Jake. The miles passed in silence as the boys retreated into themselves and their mixed emotions rambled in their thoughts, and the miles of country rolled by.

It was early afternoon when the wagon pulled in at the warehouse in Bendton. The office agent emerged to the front walk at the sound of the wagon's approach. He and Jake saw to the unloading of the boys' luggage first, then went about their business as the horses shook their traces, impatient to be rid of them. The boys grabbed their trunk, rifle, and drum to go as far as the town's main street before gaining their bearings to move on.

"Jest git us ta the corner an we'll think from ther," Duane puffed as they moved awkwardly down the dusty side street.

"Swing around left," Jonah instructed. "There's a walkway about two paces, then a step up."

With one hand gripping the trunk's leather handle and the drum slung over his shoulder, Duane felt his way with his guide stick in his free hand. Cautiously the two mounted the wooden walk, then set their burden down.

"Let's set a spell whilst I fix in ma mind where we is," the older boy instructed.

The two presented a strange sight as they sat on the corner in the middle of the sidewalk, forcing pedestrian traffic to move around them. People stared at these young strangers—a rather peculiar pair. One was a Yankee, too young to be a real soldier, and the other was a blind youth in a Rebel uniform.

"Where do we go from here?" Jonah asked.

"I figg'r the best place ta begin is Marshall Fowler's office," Duane considered.

"Where is that from here?"

"Gimme a minute." The boy searched his memory for the lay of the street. "Face ta the east down the street."

"All right," the younger boy turned.

"Da ya see the hotel?"

"Yeh."

"The marshall's office should be 'cross from it an' down a piece."

"Okay. I think I see it. But I don't know how we'll get this trunk down there in all the traffic."

"Yer right," Duane agreed.

Jonah glanced about.

"Wait here," he instructed, then was gone.

Duane sat, self-conscious of the stares he knew were on the faces of each whose footfalls passed beside him. A light rig rattled to a stop beside the walk and a light-weight figure bounced down from its seat.

"This here's Mrs. Parsons," Jonah's voice announced. "She was just coming out from the millinery store and said she would leave our trunk at the marshall's office after she finished picking up some things at the general store."

"Thank ya, Ma'am. Yer mighty kind," Duane said.

"Here, give me a hand." Jonah reached for one strap as Duane stood and took the other.

The woman helped give instructions as to where to place the trunk on the back of her vehicle, then bade the two farewell.

"I'll meet ya ta the marshall's in a half hour," she informed. "Gee up," she slapped the reins.

The light wheels of the one-horse buggy crunched softly in the dust as Mrs. Parsons pulled away to cross the street to the store.

"Come on," Jonah instructed. "Give me your arm and we can move faster."

The office was just over two blocks off. Most people gave the boys clear passage, yet twice Duane felt his friend deliberately knocked against him by someone who disliked his uniform. No words were exchanged, but he heard the mutterings of the culprits after they had walked on behind.

No one extended any kindness. Perhaps it was because of Jonah's presence. They seemed to frown their disapproval at these two strangers in their midst because they were a pair from opposite sides. What true Southerner would have a Yankee for a friend.

Suddenly, opposite the street from the marshall's there was a wild commotion as a large dog raised its head from where it lay at the office door, then sprang to its feet barking in a loud frenzy, and charged excitedly across the street.

"Stop!" a panicked youth called as he burst from the office door to see what was wrong.

Traffic hauled up short to avoid striking the animal that darted into the street toward the boys.

"Git 'em, dog!" someone shouted in anticipation of a blood bath soon to follow. "Good riddance ta Yankee trash an' turn-coats!"

"Look out!" Jonah screamed as the great canine leaped into the air onto Duane.

Forewarned, Duane turned to face the attack and put an instinctive arm across his throat. The impact threw him back against Jonah who fell beneath him as the three went crashing to the wooden walk. Women screamed and those nearby ran away in fear. Some shouted encouragement to the dog as a thirteen-year-old youth ran from the marshall's office to call off the animal.

Duane felt a large tongue bathe his face in ecstatic joy.

"It's okay, Jonah!" he cried with joyful recognition. "It's my dog! He reached his arm about the great furry neck and hugged it tightly. "Pounder!" he cried, the tears pouring down his face. "Oh, Pounder, ya knows me! I missed ya so! God, I love ya!"

Jonah crawled on his back, pushing himself free of the frenzied reunion to sit against the wall of the storefront. Duane slipped free of the drum and rolled on the ground with his dog, hugging and kissing the bulky beast which in turn bathed him in a profusion of wet kisses as well. The boy who approached from the office stopped dead in his tracks as he stared at the sight before him and exchanged quizzical glances at Jonah. In a moment he realized what was happening when he heard the boy call the dog's name.

"Dee!" Joy lit his face as he watched the two rolling in the dirt. "God, it's really you!"

"Hi, Jamie!" Duane called from beneath his dog. "Okay! Okay! It's me, Boy! Kin I git up?"

The dog stepped back, prancing with excitement, to allow his master to push himself to his hands and knees and brush away the dirt.

"You know each other?" Jonah asked, working his own way to his feet and picking up the blanketed rifle as he stood.

"Sher do," Duane said. "Jonah, this here's Jamie Fowler."

"Howdy," Jamie greeted. He turned to study his friend. "But . . ."

"I knows. I'm blind." It was a frank statement.

Pounder continued to prance and whine while Duane regained his feet and Jamie bent to retrieve the drum. Jonah found the walking stick and pressed it into Duane's hand.

"How's Pa?" Duane asked.

The boys and the dog started across the street to the office as disappointed spectators turned to go about their own business.

"Yer pa's okay," Jamie began. "Boy, is he gonna be glad ta see ya! Ya ain't knowin the hurt he's felt thinkin at fi'st ya was dead, then gittin yer letter an wonderin if'n ya'd come back safe."

"Where kin I find him?"

They were at the steps, climbing to the front porch.

"He's out ta the farm. Bin workin hard ta fixin it up agin."

The four entered the office, Pounder staying close to his master, his nose busy smelling his clothing.

"Here, have a seat." Jamie cleared a bench near the front door and motioned for both to be seated. He left the drum at the end of the bench, out of the way.

The dog lay at their feet, resting his muzzle on the toe of Duane's shoe.

"Pa's gone on his rounds," Jamie explained. "He sher 'll be su'pris'd when he gits back!" Parking himself in his father's chair, the boy continued, "I sher neve' 'spected ta see ya 'gin."

"It's bin a long time," Duane responded. "Is the office like it use ta be?"

"Pretty much so, I guess." Jamie stared at his friend. "What were it like?" he asked.

Duane reached down to scratch Pounder's ears. "I guess it were adventure at fi'st," he reflected. "Some I was lonely. Some I were scairt. When I's bin ta home fer a bit I'll come in an tell ya all 'bout it." Sensing the quiet figure at his side, he added, "Jonah here's bin 'bout the most important friend these past weeks. He's bin ma eyes so fer ta git me home."

"Hi," Jonah spoke, a lost loneliness in his voice.

"When Pa gits back we kin ride out ta yer place an' find yer pa," Jamie offered. "He's sher ta be 'bout the happiest man in the county this day." Jamie rocked back in the chair, the spring squeaking as it complained of the pressure. "We went ta see him one day afta yer letter come. He took us ta the fishin hole in the meada an' said as how he'd made a promise ther jest a'fer leavin ta the war. Somethin ta do with you, Dee."

"Yeh," the boy responded as he thought back to the night he had first known his pa would be leaving. "We walked down ther the night he said as he was goin. Pa said thet when the war was ov'r, we'd go down ther ta git the big'un."

For a moment, no more was said. Jonah was becoming increasingly uncomfortable as he felt more and more like an outsider. He began to wiggle his feet and glance about the office. Pounder seemed to sense this and to sense as well an importance in the younger boy's relation to his master. The fingers were still that had scratched his ears, as the hand rested quietly on his head. Carefully, the dog slipped away, crawling to the next figure on the bench. Then, sitting close at his feet, the dog pushed his muzzle beneath Jonah's hands and was rewarded with a vigorous rubbing of his neck and a kiss on his nose.

"You're a good friend, Pounder," he whispered.

"What will be done for Jonah?" Jamie asked, suddenly remembering the boy's presence.

"It's fer sher my pa 'n yers kin he'p us ta do right fer him," Duane replied. "Ya ain't got no worry, Jonah," he assured. "We's gonna see ta the best. Yer ma friend an my pa'll let ya stay with us fer now. I jest knows he will."

"Thanks," Jonah said. For the first time since early morning, he began to feel he wasn't to be forgotten.

"Mind if I tries yer drum?" Jamie asked.

"No, go ahead. The sticks are here in the strap." Duane felt for the strap, running his hand around the rim of the instrument near his feet, then stood to take it toward his friend's voice.

"I'll get it," Jonah volunteered, his old enthusiasm back in his voice once again.

The boy slipped the strap from Duane's hand as he stood, stepped around Pounder, and strode across the office. Jamie stood to put it over his head, then walked to the front of the desk to lean against the corner while he tapped at the drumhead with an awkward lack of beat.

Jonah wandered about, exploring the office while Duane tried to explain to Jamie just how to hold the sticks. Pounder returned to Duane's side and sat with his head on the youth's knee. An air of contentment settled in the room as the boys passed the time, awaiting the marshall's return.

*   *   *

Marshall Jonathan Fowler was overwhelmed with the joyful discovery of Duane's return. After the trunk was delivered through the kindness of Mrs. Parsons, the man gathered the boys together, locked up the office, and walked everyone around to the Fowler home. There was a brief reunion with the Fowler family over milk and fresh-baked cookies while the marshall and his son hitched the team to the wagon. Then the boys and their gear were loaded with

Pounder taking his traditional post, behind and to the center of the seat bench. A great deal of excitement and barking accompanied the departure of the wagon as it pulled out toward the Kinkade farm. Mrs. Fowler and her daughters waved the menfolk on their way, then returned to the house to prepare a late dinner for when the marshall returned. It had been agreed that the Kinkades and Jonah were to spend the night with them so that all could share in the celebration of Duane's return from the war.

Just as the wagon was leaving town, Duane asked for a brief stop along the way. Pausing at the cemetery, he asked Jonah to guide him to his mother's grave.

"It seems it was ta the northeast corner," the older boy directed.

"I think I see it," Jonah said. "Your dog has gone ahead and is waiting there."

When the two caught up to Pounder, the boy confirmed that he had guessed right. The dog sat quietly. Duane knelt down to touch the coarse grass and to run his fingers over the lettering of the headstone. Satisfied, he sat back on his heels.

"I'm home, Ma," he said. "Me 'n Pounder is here an Pa's back, too. I reckon Pa's bin by ta see ya. I want ya ta know a friend a mine from the war. His name is Jonah. He got me home.

"I sherly do miss ya, Ma. We're goin on ta see Pa. Then I'll be back ta bring ya some flowers from the meada."

Duane stood. Tears glistened in his eyes. He paused a moment to regain control of his feelings before returning to the wagon.

"Come on, Pounder," he called softly. "It's time ta go home." Reaching in search of his friend he added, "We kin go back now, Jonah."

Duane returned to the wagon with his dog and his friend to finish his journey homeward.

It was late in the afternoon as the wagon neared the farm. The end was near. Duane felt the excitement mount within as it rattled along through the afternoon's warmth. Hurry! he thought inside. The tingling ran within once more. Finally he felt the wagon turn into the lane and heard its wheels rumble across the wooden planks of the little bridge.

"Whoa," Marshall Fowler drew on the reins. The wagon came to rest in the farmyard.

"Pa!" Duane called. But there was no answer, only an open silence.

"He might be down ta the meada, Dee," Jonathan suggested.

"Jonah, would ya take me ther?"

"Sure."

"Jest folla the lane from where the barn once was," Jamie instructed. "Ya cain't miss it."

"Thanks," Jonah acknowledged as the marshall helped Duane from the wagon and passed him his walking stick.

Pounder jumped down and pranced in circles, eager to go.

"We'll be here when ya git back," the man called after them.

Duane put a hand on Jonah's shoulder and followed close at his side. "Stay close, Pounder," he called.

The dog had run ahead to the beginning of the lane. He stopped and stood panting, waiting for the two to catch up. Jamie Fowler and his father watched from the wagon as Duane and his young guide moved on down the lane, growing smaller in the distance.

The fragrance of the cultivated fields and the approaching woodland caressed the boy's nose as he thought back for a moment to the last time he had walked along this path with his pa. The two continued beyond the rows of young corn to pass under the canopy of pines that arched overhead. Soon they arrived where the path opened from the woods into the meadow with its scattered coloring of wild flowers. Beyond, the stream coursed its way to ripple across the rocks into the pool beneath the overhanging oak.

Andrew Kinkade was standing there, silently watching the ever-widening rings where a catfish had broken the water's surface.

"Is he ther?" Duane asked, breathless for an answer.

"Yes, he's there," Jonah stated.

Suddenly it was over. The years of conflict and wandering in far-away places and the loss of people so important in those times past, had fallen away into a distant memory. The search had ended.

Duane turned to his young friend with tears flooding his eyes, and grabbed him in an emotional embrace. "I'm home, Jonah! I cain't b'lieve it's really ov'r!"

The boy felt warmed yet embarrassed, too, as dampness soaked through his shirt and his own eyes welled up with his own feelings of emptiness over his father's absence. Standing free once again, the older youth brushed the tears from his face with a sweep of his sleeve.

"Jest point me in the right direction, Jonah, an' hold ma stick fer now."

The boy did as he was asked. While tears coursed down his cheeks unseen by the older youth, Jonah took Duane's arm to face him toward the figure beneath the tree.

"He's right in front of you, under the tree," Jonah explained, attempting to control his voice and to keep his own pain hidden.

The boy let go and stood quietly aside as Duane stepped forward, into the sunlight.

With Pounder at his side, allowing his master's hand to rest on his head for guidance, the two started slowly across the meadow.

The man sensed the movement off in the grass, turned his head, and saw the boy and the dog walking toward him.

Puzzled at first, he wondered who the stranger was that walked beside his son's dog. Turning for a better view, he shaded his eyes to study the pair. Suddenly, he knew! It was his own son, grown in years, taller, very different from the little boy he'd left behind. Excitement raced through his mind. Yes, it really was his son! He was alive! He had come home! He was walking toward him in the meadow! Oh, God! It's really him!

Andrew Kinkade had broken into a run as his emotions erupted from deep within. Pounder was barking excitedly.

"Dee!" the man called, a flood of tears nearly blinding him as he ran.

"Pa! Pa! I'm home!" Duane called, his joy echoing across the fields and bouncing from the trees.

The boy and his father reached each other, pulling together in a tear-filled embrace. The man swept his son off his feet. The dog circled the two, barking ecstatically, dancing joyously.

In the quiet of the tree-shadowed path, Jonah watched, and cried.

POST SCRIPTS

Through the combined efforts of Duane's father and Marshall Fowler, Jonah was reunited with his father in Pennsylvania in September of 1864. It was learned that the sutler had fully recovered from the injuries that had hospitalized him.

Nine months after Duane's return home, on April 9, 1865, General Lee surrendered his army at Appomattox Court House in Virginia. The Civil War was ended.

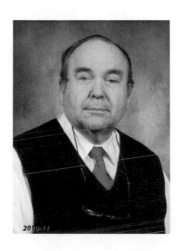

About the author, J. Arthur Moore

J. Arthur Moore is an educator with 42 years experience in public, private, and independent settings. He is also an amateur photographer and has illustrated his works with his own photographs. In addition to *Journey into Darkness*, Mr. Moore has written *Summer of Two Worlds*, "Heir to Balmawr", a drama for his fifth grade students, a number of short pieces, and short stories. His latest work is a short story titled "West to Freedom."

A graduate of Jenkintown High School, just outside of Philadelphia, Pennsylvania, he attended West Chester State College, currently West Chester University. Upon graduation, he joined the Navy and was stationed in Norfolk, Virginia, where he met his wife to be, a widow with four children. Once discharged from the service, he moved to Coatesville, Pennsylvania, began his teaching career, married and brought his new family to live in a 300-year-old farm house in which the children grew up and married, went their own ways, raised their families to become grandparents themselves.

Retiring after a 42-year career, Mr. Moore has moved to the farming country in Lancaster County, Pennsylvania, where he plans to enjoy the generations of family and time with his model railroad, and time to guide his writings into a new life through publication. It also allows time for traveling to Civil War events, presenting at various organizations and events, time with adopted grandchildren (five former students who were key to the 6-month move project and have become family), and, having saved the camp equipment from years of programs with schools and in the summer, the chance to build a camp site in the back yard for the kids.

Edwards Brothers Malloy
Thorofare, NJ USA
April 15, 2013